EDGAR ALLAN'S OFFICIAL CRIME INVESTIGATION NOTEBOOK

Mary Amato

Holiday House / New York

HOLIDAY HOUSE is registered in the U.S. Patent and Trademark Office.
Printed and Bound in November 2012 at Maple Press, York, PA, USA.
The text typeface is ITC Slimbach Book.
www.holidayhouse.com

7 9 10 8 6

Library of Congress Cataloging-in-Publication Data

Amato, Mary.
Edgar Allan's official crime investigation notebook /
by Mary Amato. — 1st ed.
Summary: When someone takes a pet goldfish then other items from
Ms. Herschel's classroom, each time leaving a clue in the form
of a poem, student Edgar Allan competes with a classmate
to be first to solve the mystery.
ISBN 978-0-8234-2271-5 (hardcover)
[1. Mystery and detective stories.   2. Lost and found possessions—Fiction.
3. Teachers—Fiction.   4. Schools—Fiction.   5. Poetry—Fiction.]   I. Title.
PZ7.A49165Edg 2010
[Fic]—dc22
2010011604

ISBN 978-0-8234-2386-6 (paperback)

For all the people who have shared
the love of poetry with me, especially Mrs. Chattin;
Mrs. Osborne; Mr. McCauley; Frau Hildebrandt;
Mr. Osborne; Mari Vlastos; Natasha Saje;
David Christman; Julie Lowins Zielke;
Andrew Schindel; Jed Feffer; Richard Washer;
Phyllis Mentzell Ryder; Ivan,
Sol, and Sylvia Amato;
and my kids.

CHAPTER ONE

The classroom was as dark and quiet as an old graveyard at dawn. The thief crept in, taped a mysterious message on the board, tiptoed to the Pet Corner, and peered at the fish.

You're mine now, the thief thought with a sly smile.

At Wordsworth Elementary School, just before the day began, someone stole the fish from the tank in Ms. Herschel's fifth-grade classroom. Now the fifth graders were gathered around the message left on the board, everyone talking at once.

Well, not everyone. One student, Edgar Allan, wasn't saying a word. He had his eyes closed and was imagining what the ordeal must have been like for the fish. He could almost feel the rushing of the water against his fins and tail as he was being lifted out. Edgar wasn't sure how fish brains worked, but he bet the fish was scared.

"Please close your mouths and take your seats," Ms. Herschel said. "We won't get anywhere with all this noise." Their teacher set down her coffee cup, sat on the edge of her desk, and looked at her students over the rims of her dark-framed glasses, waiting for them to settle down.

As Edgar walked to his desk, a shiver rippled through him. A strange chill always lingers at the scene of a robbery, even after the thief has gone, and Edgar could feel it in the air. He sat and looked at his classmates. Everyone was sitting quietly, except for a skinny boy named Kip, whose leg was jiggling against his desk, and Taz, the tallest in the class, who was pretending to swim to his seat in the last row while making fish faces.

"Taz, do you think this is funny?" Ms. Herschel asked.

"I don't think it's funny," Maia said. "I gave Slurpy to the whole class as a gift. Whoever stole that cute little fish was mean." She tossed back her long black hair and threw a hard glance at Taz.

"Very bad," Gabriela, the new girl, quickly agreed.

"Stop staring at me," Taz said to the girls. "What do you think? I came in here and ate it for breakfast?" He laughed and made a slurping sound.

Destiny Perkins sat up taller in her seat. "Stealing anything is wrong. But stealing living things seems worse because whatever you're stealing is probably scared."

Edgar glanced at Destiny, realizing that she must have imagined what the fish was feeling, too.

"If I wanted to, I could steal something and not get caught because I'm fast," Kip said, and he was about to leap up and prove it, but Ms. Herschel stopped him.

"What if Slurpy is dead!" Maia exclaimed.

Patrick, a boy who couldn't sit straighter if he tried, raised his hand. "I think Slurpy was stolen, not murdered, because of what the note says. The thief left clues in it."

"Interesting, Patrick," Ms. Herschel said. "Would you like to read the note aloud?"

Even though Ms. Herschel had said nothing about using her pointer, Patrick walked to the board, picked up the teacher's wooden stick, and pointed to each line in the note as he read it aloud.

Thief

The thief comes
on little cat feet

sits looking
at the goldfish
then takes it carefully
and moves on.

"See the title?" Patrick pointed. "Thief. Not murderer! And the thief takes the fish *carefully*."

"A cat did it!" Kip said.

Maia rolled her eyes. "The thief is *like* a cat, meaning sneaky." She threw another look at Taz.

"I think you're right about the thief being sneaky, Maia," Ms. Herschel said. "But let's not jump to conclusions about who did it without more clues."

"Maybe none of us did it," Destiny said. "Maybe it was a professional thief."

An invisible finger of ice touched Edgar's spine. A

professional thief! He opened his notebook and began writing.

> Tuesday, October 2
> My whole body is shivering. A criminal has been in this very room where I'm now sitting. All my life I've been waiting for something like this to happen.
> I'll record clues in this notebook. I will catch this thief before anyone else does!

Excited, he closed the notebook and wrote in big letters on the front:

> Edgar Allan's Official
> Crime Investigation Notebook

Still standing at the front, Patrick pulled a silver camera out of his pocket. "Ms. Herschel, may I take a picture of the evidence?"

"Great idea, Patrick," Ms. Herschel said. "But then I'm afraid we really have to begin our science lesson."

Edgar couldn't believe his ears or eyes.

> Ms. Herschel is letting Patrick takes pictures of the crime scene.
> This is not fair. Some of us do not have cameras.
> Never fear! I will design a trap

to catch the thief. I will put a
fake fish in the tank with a string
attached. When the thief takes
the fish, the string will pull on
a net that falls down from the
ceiling.

As Patrick strolled by Edgar's desk on his way to his own, he grabbed Edgar's notebook and started to read it.

"Give it back!" Edgar whispered angrily.

Patrick scribbled a message and tossed it back to Edgar.

Your trap is stupid.

Edgar glared at his classmate who was now busy writing on the cover of his own notebook. When Edgar leaned over to see what he was writing, he almost fell off his chair.

Patrick just wrote "Patrick
Chen's Official Crime Investigation
Notebook" on his notebook, which
is basically stealing my idea, so
who is the criminal now?

He covered his notebook with his arm so Patrick couldn't get another glimpse.

Patrick leaned over and whispered, "What a crime solver needs is a theory about why someone would commit the crime. I've got one. Do you?"

"Of course," Edgar said. Then he hunched over his desk and wrote:

> Help! I need a theory. Why? Why? Why steal a small, goldish red fish with a white belly that bothered no one and gave joy to the happy students at Wordsworth Elementary School?
>
> All I know is there are criminals out there who do bad things and innocent fish pay the price.

CHAPTER TWO

Edgar's brain was bubbling, and a theory was finally coming to the surface.

"Time for math," Ms. Herschel said. "Let's see who can solve today's math brain teaser."

Not math, Edgar thought. Not at a time like this!

While she read the day's word problem out loud, he grabbed his notebook.

> What if the thief knows something about Slurpy that we don't know? Perhaps Slurpy is a rare species, a one-of-a-kind fish, that can be sold on eBay for big bucks! Now, *that's* a theory!

Edgar raised his hand.

"That was quick problem-solving, Edgar! What's the answer?"

"I don't know. I was just wondering if I could go to the computer station and do some research on a certain important topic." He glanced at Patrick to see if he was impressed.

"No you may not. We are doing math now."

> Doesn't Ms. Herschel know that asking me to stop investigating is like asking a fly to stop flying or a bee to stop beeing or a cheetah to stop cheeting?

Ms. Herschel repeated the word problem. "Two years ago my dog had eight puppies. I kept one-fourth of them. Last year my dog had six more puppies. I kept one-half of them. How many puppies do I have now?"

Taz raised his hand. "You'd have zero puppies because now they would all be grown-up dogs!"

Ms. Herschel had to laugh. "Well, you're right. Okay, how many *dogs* do I have now?"

Patrick and Destiny raised their hands at the same time. Before their teacher could choose who to call on, Patrick blurted out the answer. "One-quarter of eight is two, plus half of six is three, so you would have five dogs plus the mother dog."

"Good problem-solving, Patrick!" Ms. Herschel said. "Now, I'll put four new problems up on the board and set the timer. See if you can get all four done before the timer rings."

> Patrick is smart. I'm afraid he's going to solve the crime before me. It'll be like the science fair all over

again. Patrick brought that recy-
cling robot that crushed empty cans
and lit up. All I brought was a rock.
   Okay it was a very nice smooth
rock and my question was what
makes some rocks smooth? But still
it was just a rock.

The room was silent, except for the scratching of pencils on paper and the sound of Kip's leg jiggling against
his desk. Everyone was working on the math problems,
except Taz, who was playing with a keychain.

Edgar had a sudden urge to blow his nose. As he
walked up to get a tissue, he stopped by Maia's desk and
whispered, "What kind of goldfish was Slurpy?"

She looked up from her math work and whispered
back. "He was an ordinary goldfish, Edgar."

"How do you know?" he asked.

"My mom is the manager of Pet Place," she whispered.

"I got my iguana at Pet Place!" Sammy said.

"Edgar," Ms. Herschel called out. "You're wasting
time and distracting others."

Disappointed, he took a tissue and blew his nose. On
his way back to his seat, he glanced at the Pet Corner,
which was in the back, by the sink. The empty tank on
the counter, where Slurpy had been, looked as sad as a
box of chocolates after all the chocolates are gone. In a
cage next to it, Mister Furball, the hamster, popped out of
a toilet paper roll and began sniffing around. Edgar tried
to lock eyes with Mister Furball, but Ms. Herschel told
him to sit down and get to work.

> There is one person who I'm
> sure witnessed the crime and could
> tell me the name of the criminal!
> Unfortunately that person is a
> hamster.

He tried working on math, but a new theory was gnawing away at his mind. What if the thief was interested in stealing all kinds of pets, not just fish? He might return to the scene of the crime and steal poor Mister Furball! Maybe the thief was still here, hiding somewhere in the school—in a closet—and he was planning the next theft at this moment.

Realizing that his pencil needed sharpening, Edgar raced to the sharpener, which happened to be near the Pet Corner. While sharpening, he looked at Mister Furball's cage. Perhaps he could build a trap that would catch the thief and save Mister Furball. Certainly no one else in the room had thought of this. Edgar glanced at himself in the mirror that was over the sink, to see if he looked as distinguished as he felt. Unfortunately, he hadn't grown any taller, and he had slept on his thick brown hair so it was sticking up in the back, but his big brown eyes looked full of daring and his feathery eyebrows could do wonderful things on command.

Fired up, he bolted to Ms. Herschel's desk and whispered, "May I be excused from doing math so I can immediately build a hamster protection device?"

"No, Edgar. You have to do the math like everyone else."

Only temporarily discouraged, an even more brilliant thought popped into his head. "If you bring in one of your puppies, I'll train it as a classroom guard dog!"

"I don't have any puppies, Edgar. That was just a word problem."

Crushed, Edgar sat back down. Mister Furball was standing on his hind legs with his little paws on the bars, looking right at him.

Never fear, Mister Furball! I will ask Mr. Crew to let me skip language arts to do a complete search of the school. Unlike Ms. Herschel, Mr. Crew has a heart.

Edgar wasn't positive, but he thought he saw Mister Furball smile.

CHAPTER THREE

On the way from Ms. Herschel's room to Mr. Crew's room, where Edgar had language arts, there was a janitorial supply closet big enough to hide a thief and his loot. Edgar walked toward it quickly. There was no guarantee the thief would be hiding inside, but Edgar was not about to pass by a possible hideout and leave it unchecked. The secret was to stay one step ahead of Patrick.

Kip was already at Mr. Crew's door, but his other classmates were behind Edgar, which would mean they would witness how smart he was to think of investigating the closet. He reached the door, turned the knob, and opened it, ready to duck if the thief had a weapon.

A push from behind sent Edgar stumbling into the little room. The door slammed shut, plunging him into total darkness. He reeled around, yelling and groping for the door. "Help!" He banged on the door. "Help!"

The door flew open, and Clarice Stolnup was standing there, laughing her head off. Clarice was a small blond girl in the other class who had a large mouth, mean eyes, and a passion for making other people miserable. Edgar avoided her whenever possible.

"What were you looking for?" Clarice said. "Toilet paper?"

"That wasn't funny, Clarice," Destiny said, but Edgar was sure he heard some other people laughing.

Embarrassed, he hurried on to Mr. Crew's room. By the time he walked in, Patrick was already standing at the teacher's desk, showing him the thief's message on the viewing screen of his camera.

"This is fascinating, Patrick!" Mr. Crew was exclaiming, his eyes dancing like candle flames on a chocolate birthday cake. Their language arts teacher was genuinely fascinated about most things, which was why his students loved him. "This message is like a poem. The thief is using the image of a cat to describe himself or herself."

"Maia said that!" Gabriela exclaimed.

"Good job, Maia," Mr. Crew stepped over to Maia's desk for a high five. "That's called a metaphor. How lucky! I was going to start our unit on poetry today, and now I can use this as a springboard. We can start with metaphor."

"I know who the criminal is," Patrick said.

"Really?" Mr. Crew stroked his black mustache. "Well, make sure you have solid evidence before you go pointing a finger, Patrick."

Patrick showed Mr. Crew his crime investigation notebook. "I'm already working on that."

Edgar sat down, disappointed.

I can't even ask Mr. Crew about leaving his room to search the school because Patrick is hogging all the space up there. I will wait until everybody is working and Mr. Crew is alone at his desk. Then I'll make my move.

"Okay, everybody!" Mr. Crew pulled his chair over to the board and hopped up on it. "Kip, will you hand me that paintbrush and that can of paint?"

"What for?"

"Watch!" He took the paintbrush from Kip, dipped it in the paint, and wrote in big letters on the wall above the board.

A POEM IS A GIFT.

"I'd rather have candy," Kip said.

"I'd rather have a new soccer ball," Sammy said.

"I'd rather have Slurpy back," Maia said.

Edgar had always wanted a dog, but now that the idea of a guard dog had leaped into his mind, he wanted one more than ever.

Mr. Crew gave the paintbrush back to Kip and hopped down from his stool. "I hope by the end of this unit, you'll all come to enjoy poetry. Who thinks they know what I mean by saying a poem is a gift?"

Maia raised her hand. "The writer of the poem is giving it to the world like a beautiful gift."

"What if it's an ugly poem?" Taz said and laughed.

"I don't think every poem has to be beautiful," Destiny

said. "You can write a sad poem. If you write a poem to express yourself, then it's a gift to yourself."

"That's a terrific way to put it." Mr. Crew smiled, and his mustache smiled, too.

"Mr. Crew, I got a question," Taz said. "Why didn't you just write it on the board like a normal teacher?"

Mr. Crew laughed. "I'm writing it on the wall because I don't want it to get erased. I want you to remember it. A poem is a gift."

Taz put one hand over his heart and sang,

> *Happy birthday to me.*
> *Don't give me a flea*
> *all covered with chocolate...*
> *or I'll stick you in a tree.*

Mr. Crew laughed again. "See? Taz made us laugh with his poem. That was a gift."

Patrick scribbled something down in his crime notebook. Edgar noticed and couldn't help wondering what it was.

"Hey, Mr. Crew," Taz said. "How come you can write on the wall, but if we do we get in trouble?"

Mr. Crew laughed. "I got permission from the principal. Try that next time. Now, back to metaphor." Mr. Crew pulled his chair to his desk. "Who remembers what that means?"

"A metaphor is when you use one thing to describe another, like the thief is a cat," Maia said.

"Or happiness is a flower," Gabriela suggested.

"Yes!"

"I don't get it," Kip said.

"Think of candy," Destiny suggested, and Kip's eyes lit up. "Then think of something else that's really fun, like a party. Then squash the two things together: Candy is a party in my mouth. That's a metaphor."

"Nice one, Destiny," Mr. Crew said. "So here's what we're going to do. We're each going to think of a subject that we want to write about, then come up with a metaphor to use, like the thief is a cat, and write a poem."

"Can we work with a partner?" Maia asked.

"Sure, but before you start, I'm going to make you sit for two minutes in absolute silence to let your ideas and thoughts come out. Think of your imagination as a seed; silence is the water that helps it to grow."

The moment the room grew quiet, Edgar walked up to Mr. Crew's desk.

"Edgar, it's time to sit and think," Mr. Crew whispered.

Edgar lowered his voice as far as it would go. "But I really need to search the school. I have reason to believe the thief might strike again."

Mr. Crew nodded. "I see. But if I let you go, then I'd have to agree to let everyone go. And if everyone went, we wouldn't get any poetry writing done."

"I can live with that," Edgar whispered.

"Tell you what. Write a poem. Maybe if we have a minute or two left at the end, and if you have a specific place you'd like to search, I'll consider it."

Edgar walked back to his seat.

Big problem. I don't have any
ideas. I don't even like poetry.
These teachers who expect us to

16

concentrate when there's a thief
running loose are crazy.

    Sometimes when I look at a blank
piece of paper, my stomach hurts.

    Mr. Crew just said if we don't
get a poem finished in class he
wants us to do it tonight. The pres-
sures are piling up.

"Would anyone like to share a poem before we get dismissed for lunch?" Mr. Crew asked.

Maia raised her hand. She and Gabriela read the poem they had written together.

Goldfish
Underneath dark water
A fish is dancing light.
When the light goes out
The day becomes night.

"That was terrific, girls!" Mr. Crew exclaimed. "Light is a metaphor for a goldfish! And what do you think they mean by 'When the light goes out the day becomes night?' "

"They're saying it's sad when the fish disappears," Patrick offered.

"Yes! Beautiful! Who wants to go next?"

Kip was practically jumping out of his seat. "I wrote one about my skateboard," he said.

My Skateboard
My board is a bird
and I ride on its back.

We fly out of half pipes
and get lots of air.
When I do a 360
and grab the nose,
then my bird
is my flying chair.

"Fantastic! Love it! Two metaphors—your board is a bird and a chair! Bravo!" Mr. Crew looked like he was going to explode with happiness. "Who's next?"

Taz raised his hand. Edgar was amazed. Was he the only one who was having trouble concentrating?

"Mine is about my dog," Taz said with a grin.

Dog Breath
A monster lives inside my dog
Its smell is worse than death.
It comes out when he kisses me
Its name is Big Bad Breath.

While the class was laughing and Mr. Crew was giving Taz a standing ovation, Patrick wrote another entry in his crime notebook. Edgar watched him nervously.

> I didn't get anything done in this stupid class. No good observations. No poem. I am a failure. I am giving up.

CHAPTER FOUR

"Don't get any closer!" Patrick yelled. "I'm documenting some important evidence."

Recess just went from bad to worse. Patrick was busy and official, aiming his camera at a shoe print in the mud. The girls were gathered around him.

"Do you think that's the shoe print of the thief?" Maia asked.

Patrick checked the picture in his viewfinder. "I'm going to present my evidence to the whole class after I have analyzed everything."

"It's Taz, isn't it?" Maia said. "He thinks everything is one big joke."

"Well, he might not be laughing when I'm done." Patrick looked up at Edgar. "I've already done two interviews to verify the exact time of the crime and have come up with some important conclusions. What have you done?"

Edgar walked away.

"I'm going to crack this case!" Patrick called after him.

Patrick's voice pierced, but Edgar fought to keep

walking steadily on, as if nothing were wrong. At the bottom of the playground, he sat down in the grass.

> I pretended I couldn't hear
> Patrick because of wax build-up in
> my ears. He has such good ideas,
> it makes my teeth hurt. But giving
> up would be like handing him a big
> bowl of victory with whipped cream
> on top.
>   Patrick seems to think it is Taz.
> I shall do an official interview
> right now and come up with some
> important conclusions of my own!
> I will ask Taz a series of brilliant
> questions and watch his eyeballs
> carefully. If he is guilty, his eyeballs
> will show it. Eyeballs never lie!

Edgar saw Taz crouched next to the tree stump on the other side of the basketball court. Trying to look nonchalant, Edgar sauntered over and stood next to him. Taz was looking at a butterfly that was resting on a blade of grass. The wings were blue with tiny dots of black and white and red along each edge.

> OFFICIAL INTERVIEW
> WITH TAZ RASKEL
> EDGAR: I have a question for you.
> TAZ: My mom said I shouldn't
>   talk to strangers.

EDGAR: I'm not a stranger.

TAZ: You're stranger than you
         think! Ha ha ha.

EDGAR: When <u>exactly</u> did you
         arrive at school today?

TAZ: I got here at <u>exactly</u> the
         time I got here.

EDGAR: Which was when?

TAZ: Which was when I got
         here. Ha ha ha!

EDGAR: That's not really an
         answer.

TAZ: It was a joke, lil mystery
         dude.

EDGAR: Oh. Please just call me
         mystery dude.

TAZ: Okay lil mystery dude.

EDGAR: I have another question. Do
         you or do you not like fish?

TAZ: Only on a bun with tartar
         sauce.

TAZ WITH PIZAZZ WAZ HERE.

IMPORTANT CONCLUSION:
   Do not stand too close to Taz
when you are interviewing or he
will take your pencil and write in
your notebook.

The bell rang, signaling the end of recess.

"Hey Edgar, does this wing look like it got a rip in it?" Taz asked.

Edgar crouched and looked. The butterfly was opening and closing its wings but not taking off.

"I hope you're okay, lil butterfly guy," Taz said.

During recess today, Taz showed concern for a seriously wounded butterfly. Not what you'd expect from a criminal. Perhaps he is doing this to throw me off. I will superglue myself to Taz's side. If he is hiding something, I will find it out in the next hour or my name isn't Edgar Allan.

CHAPTER FIVE

When the bell rang, announcing the end of recess, Taz raced inside. Edgar ran after him, staying just far enough away that Taz wouldn't see him. Where was he going in such a hurry? Perhaps he wanted to steal something from another teacher before the afternoon classes started, Edgar thought.

Taz turned down the hall toward the main office. With his short legs, Edgar had to walk extra fast to keep up. By the time he arrived in the office, Taz was behind the counter asking Mrs. Peabody a question.

"I understand. Certainly, Taz," Mrs. Peabody was saying. "Here you go." She handed the phone to Taz.

Who was Taz calling in the middle of the school day, Edgar wondered?

"It's like Grand Central Station in here!" Mrs. Peabody said. "Edgar, what do you need?"

"Um," Edgar glanced at a student who was sitting in a chair with an ice pack on his head. "I was wondering if you have a tissue? My nose is running."

Mrs. Peabody handed Edgar a tissue. "Go to class."

"Hi Mom, it's me," Taz said into the phone. "I was just wondering if you had any news...I know, it's just that I can't stop thinking about it....Okay...okay...bye."

When Taz handed the phone back to Mrs. Peabody, he looked upset. He rushed past Edgar, out the door.

"Mrs. Peabody, what was Taz talking about?" Edgar asked.

"I don't think that's any of your business," she said.

At that moment, Patrick popped up from behind the counter. He smiled at Edgar and then turned to Mrs. Peabody. "Thank you for letting me look through the Lost and Found box," he said. "My umbrella isn't here."

"Go to class, both of you!" Mrs. Peabody shooed them out the door.

"You're spying on Taz, too," Patrick said as they walked toward the fifth-grade hallway.

"How did you get here ahead of me? I thought I was the only one following him," Edgar said.

"At the end of language arts, I heard Taz ask Mr. Crew if he could call his mom, and Mr. Crew told him to go to the office after recess. So before recess was over, I asked permission to go to the office." He smiled. "Did you like the Lost and Found idea?"

Edgar didn't like any of it.

"I have a theory why Taz is upset. Do you?"

"Yes, I do," Edgar said. "A big theory." Actually he wasn't sure.

"What is the next phase of your investigation?" Patrick asked. "Do you even have one?"

"Yes, I do," Edgar said.

"I have an interview to do," Patrick said.

"I have an interview to do, too," Edgar said.

"Interview with who?"

Patrick asked this question just as they were passing Ms. Herschel's room. Edgar stopped and stuck his head in the door. "Ms. Herschel. May I speak with you..." He glanced back at Patrick. "In private?"

"Very briefly," Ms. Herschel said.

Edgar closed the door in Patrick's face.

OFFICIAL INTERVIEW
WITH MS. HERSCHEL

EDGAR: Ma'am, in your exact words, when exactly was Slurpy stolen?

MS. HERSCHEL: Edgar, I appreciate how seriously you're taking this, but I already went over the story.

EDGAR: I need to establish the exact time of the crime, ma'am. What time did you arrive at work?

MS. HERSCHEL: You can call me Ms. Herschel, Edgar. Like I said, the fish was here when I arrived at 7:45. At 8:20, I

```
                         went to get some
                         coffee. When I
                         came back at 8:55,
                         it was gone.
EDGAR:                   How do you think
                         the thief got in?
MS. HERSCHEL:            Well, I left my
                         door unlocked.
EDGAR:                   I see. Does the
                         principal know
                         that you are
                         careless about
                         locking up and
                         that you are
                         drinking coffee
                         on the job, ma'am?
MS. HERSCHEL:            Go to class, Edgar.
```

IMPORTANT CONCLUSION:
   For a cup of coffee, Ms.
Herschel will risk the life of a
helpless fish.

When Edgar arrived at Mr. Crew's for the afternoon social studies lesson, Patrick whispered. "What did you interview Ms. Herschel about?"

Edgar zipped his lips and sat down. Determined to keep his powers of observation as sharp as possible, he looked around the room, on the alert for suspicious behavior.

Mr. Crew was making a cup of tea with the electric teapot he kept on his counter. Perhaps if Ms. Herschel switched to tea, he thought, there would be no more robberies.

Gabriela walked in next with a shoe box full of small wooden animals from Oaxaca, Mexico. Since they were studying Mexico, and since Gabriela had just moved from Mexico, she had mentioned her collection and Mr. Crew had asked her to bring it in.

"*¡Fantástico!*" Mr. Crew said. "Why don't you set them up on the shelf in the back."

Most of the students gathered around the bookshelf to watch Gabriela unwrap and set out each colorful piece. Edgar joined them, and Patrick followed closely.

"I hope no one steals them," Maia said. Gabriela looked worried.

"Don't worry, Gabriela," Patrick said. "I'm on it."

"These are cool," Taz said, picking up a bright blue and orange dog.

"I'm on it, too," Edgar said, but nobody heard him.

In art, which was Edgar's final class of the day, as everyone was busy painting the papier mâché masks they had made, Edgar watched Taz for signs of suspicious behavior. Taz painted a fake mustache on his own face and had to wash it off, but that was the only excitement.

While Taz was at the sink washing up, Edgar had a brainstorm. Maybe Slurpy was not the only victim. He knew for a fact that the kindergarten room had a whole tankful of goldfish! Had anyone thought to ask if another classroom was hit? Perhaps if he interviewed Ms. Barrett, the kindergarten teacher, he could come up with the evidence that would link Taz to that crime!

He glanced at Patrick who was concentrating on his mask project. Patrick probably hadn't thought of this! If Edgar acted quickly, he could be the one to solve the mystery before the school day ended.

Edgar set his paintbrush down and walked up to his art teacher's desk. "May I go to the bathroom, Ms. Cassatt?"

"It can't wait?"

"I'm afraid not," Edgar said.

She handed him a pass, and he walked out.

OFFICIAL INTERVIEW
WITH MS. BARRETT

EDGAR: May I ask you a few questions, Ms. Barrett?

MS. BARRETT: As you can see, I am right in the middle of reading a story to my class, Edgar.

EDGAR: It's a matter of life and death.

MS. BARRETT: Make it very, very quick.

EDGAR: Do you enjoy drinking coffee?

MS. BARRETT: I don't see how this can be a matter—

EDGAR: Please, ma'am. Just answer yes or no.

MS. BARRETT: Well, yes, but—

EDGAR:	Aha! And when you get your coffee, do you or do you not leave your door unlocked?
MS. BARRETT:	Edgar, what is all this about?
EDGAR:	Your missing gold-fish, ma'am.
MS. BARRETT:	None of our fish are missing.
EDGAR:	Oh.
MS. BARRETT:	Where should you be right now, Edgar?
EDGAR:	Art.
MS. BARRETT:	Go to class, Edgar.

IMPORTANT CONCLUSION:
   Ms. Barrett should smile. She is kind of mean for a kindergarten teacher and her face is getting permanent frown wrinkles.

By the time Edgar returned to the classroom, art was almost over.

"Edgar, you're falling behind," the art teacher said. "Everyone but you is ready to add the feathers and beads. I think you'll have to come in during recess tomorrow and paint."

Edgar looked around the room. The masks on every

table were screaming with bright colors. His was plain white.

"What about right now? I can do it right now," Edgar said.

"Too late." The teacher turned her attention to dismissal. Edgar put away his materials and gathered up his stuff. He went back to Ms. Herschel's room to get ready for final dismissal and wait for his bus number to be called.

"Ms. Herschel," Patrick said loudly. "Since I don't have to ride the bus, can I stay and do more investigating?"

"Great idea, Patrick," Ms. Herschel said.

"My dad is going to want to hear every detail," he went on. "He's a forensic chemist, you know. The police consult him for information about stuff like fingerprints and poison and crime stuff."

Edgar's bones rattled with jealousy. Last year in Ms. Brooks's class, Patrick's dad, Mr. Chen, came and made a mysterious powder in a test tube turn green and then explode. He was dressed in a black suit that looked like something from a James Bond movie.

"My dad is a pilot, and my mom is a lawyer," Taz said.

Ms. Herschel started asking other kids about their parents, and Edgar held his breath, hoping that if he didn't breathe much, he would be invisible and Ms. Herschel wouldn't call on him.

"What about your parents, Edgar?" Ms. Herschel said. "What do they do?"

Edgar's stomach dropped.

"They're clowns," Patrick said.

Ms. Herschel laughed. "No, really. What do they do?"

Destiny, who also remembered Edgar's parents from last year's class visit, explained that they worked in the Clown Care Unit at Children's Hospital, and that their job was to tell jokes and sing funny songs to cheer up sick kids.

Ms. Herschel said, "How wonderful," and when Edgar was a kindergartner he thought so, too. Now he wanted to crawl under a rock. Finally his bus number was called, and he ran out, climbed into his bus, and flung himself into the first seat. To his surprise, a poem popped into his mind. A metaphor poem!

Skunk
by Edgar Allan
The Skunk comes
on big stinking feet.

He takes pictures
with a fancy camera
and then
he rips your heart out.

CHAPTER SIX

For dinner that night: fish. On a bun. With tartar sauce.

Edgar looked at his plate and thought of Slurpy. He couldn't eat.

"So how was school today, boys?" Edgar's mom looked at Edgar and his older brother, Henri.

"Did you learn anything?" his dad added, shoveling a spoonful of fish mixed with mushed peas into the little mouth of Edgar's baby sister, Rosy.

Although they had taken off their costumes and clown makeup, Edgar noticed with dismay that they didn't need odd clothes or cosmetics to look like clowns. His father was extremely short, had a shiny bald head, a wide smile, and a big nose that was always somewhat reddish at the tip. His mother was tall, with tiny ruby lips, sparkling green eyes, long black eyelashes, and a shock of red hair that she wore piled on top of her head like three scoops of strawberry ice cream. To the three Allan children, they were known as dad and mom, of course, but to the rest of the world they were known by their stage names: Tubby and Twig.

Edgar summoned his most serious tone and announced that they'd had a robbery at his school.

"A robbery?" Twig put down her fork, eyelashes fluttering. "What was stolen?"

"The goldfish from Ms. Herschel's room."

Henri laughed. Even though little Rosy didn't know what was funny, she laughed, too.

"It's not funny," Edgar said.

"Sounds like the fish dropped out of school," Henri said.

Tubby and Twig roared as if it was the funniest joke on the planet. Rosy slapped her chubby hands on her high chair tray.

Twig leaned forward, her eyebrows arching, and asked: "What do you call a fish without an eye?"

"Fsh?" Henri guessed, and they laughed again.

"Anyway, I have important news," Henri announced. "Today I played so well in band, Mr. Copland said I could play a solo at the band concert." He sat up even taller, which was impressive, since he had inherited his mother's height—along with her red hair, green eyes, and double-jointed fingers.

"Congratulations, Mr. Music Man!" Tubby said.

Twig raised her glass and the three of them clinked.

"I was thinking I could do the solo for the Cabaret if you want," Henri added.

The proud parents smiled at each other. The Cabaret was a talent show that they hosted to benefit the Children's Hospital every year. "What a lovely idea," Twig said.

"Luminiferous!" Tubby agreed, sticking another spoonful of mush into Rosy's mouth.

Edgar cleared his throat. "I was thinking...if I had a dog, I could bring him to school and train him to guard things."

Henri set down his milk. "I've heard of sheep dogs, but dogs guarding fish? What do you think, Rosy? Fido the Fishdog?" Edgar's brother panted and howled at Rosy, who laughed so hard mush dribbled down her chin.

His parents couldn't help laughing, too.

Edgar scowled.

"I'm sorry, Edgar," Twig said. "We're not laughing at you."

"Well what about it?" Edgar persisted.

"A dog?" Twig shook her head. "We told you before: You kids keep us busy enough! Besides, I'm sure your teacher will make sure nothing else gets stolen."

Tubby wiped Rosy's mouth and gave her a wooden spoon to play with. She grabbed it and promptly bonked her dad on the head.

"Ouch!" Tubby said. "Maybe we should trade her in for a dog."

"We were talking about the Cabaret," Henri said. "How many friends can I invite this year?"

For the rest of dinner, Edgar's parents and Henri talked about the Cabaret. It was supposed to be fun, but Edgar found it stressful because he didn't have a talent. Last year his dad had tried to teach him how to play the accordion, but his fingers kept tripping over the buttons and he quit.

"Are you doing anything for it this year, Edgar?" Henri asked.

Edgar pushed his plate away. "No."

"Why don't you play the cowbell on the song your dad and I are doing?" Twig said.

Henri laughed. "Yeah. Play the cowbell."

Tubby gave Henri a look. "The cowbell is a great idea, right, Henri?"

"Right," Henri said, trying unsuccessfully to hide his smile.

"Which reminds me. Where do cows go to make it in show business?" Tubby asked.

"Moo York City!" Twig stood up and sang, "If I can make it there, I'll make it anywhere. No udder place than old Moo York!"

His parents started mooing in two-part harmony, Henri added rhythm by clinking his fork on his glass, and Rosy banged along with her wooden spoon. On another night, Edgar might have joined in, but he couldn't stomach it. Ever since Henri started middle school and made it into advanced band, he thought that his accomplishments should be the topic of every conversation. Now that Edgar finally had something important to talk about, nobody seemed to care. Patrick's dad was probably giving him crime-solving tips at this very moment.

"Excuse me," Edgar interrupted. "Can I use the computer to do some research?"

Henri stopped. "I already asked to use it. I have to download clarinet music for school. And I have a history report that's due first thing in the morning. "

"That's true," Tubby said. "Edgar, do you absolutely need the computer for your homework?"

Edgar sighed and shook his head. He had thought he

would look up fish facts to see if he could find some kind of clue.

To make it worse, Henri hopped up and said, "Ha! It's your turn to do the dishes, Edgar."

"Knock, knock," Tubby said.

"Who's there?" Twig asked.

"Dishes."

"Dishes who?"

Tubby stuck a carrot in his mouth like a cigar. "Dishes a very bad joke."

"You are so cute!" Twig leaned over and planted a kiss on top of her husband's bald head.

Rosy leaned forward and burped.

Edgar sighed. Could the night get any worse?

I am in the bathroom right now because I am too mad to be in the same room with anybody, and they are taking up all the good rooms. I am sitting in the bathtub with all my clothes on because I don't feel like sitting on the toilet, and there are no chairs in here.

Am I the only one who cares about Slurpy? I wonder if he is dead. Is there such a thing as a Goldfish Heaven in the clouds? Since clouds are really floating water molecules, then I suppose fishes could feel right at home in them. Maybe there are entire schools of goldfish spirits in the clouds.

Maybe Slurpy is happier being with all the other dead fish. I always thought that he looked lonely in that little tank. On the other hand, Mister Furball kept him company. Maybe they stayed up late and did tricks for each other. It would be nice to have a friend like that.

I just had a bad fantasy.

I imagined that I walked into Ms. Herschel's room and found Mister Furball gone. I said, "The thief has struck again!" and everybody looked at me and said, "Oh no!" and here's the bad part...it was exciting! I <u>want</u> Mister Furball to get stolen!

A nice person wouldn't want an innocent hamster to be the second victim in a dramatic crime wave.

I just really really want to solve a mystery. Everybody has something they're good at except me. This could be my thing.

Through the crack under the bathroom door, the sound of Henri's clarinet music drifted in. His parents had joined him on the ukelele and accordion. Through the bathroom window, which was open slightly, he heard the groan of his neighbor's car starting and farther off, the sound of a siren.

Edgar imagined being very high up, as high as a cloud. He imagined floating up there, like the spirit of a goldfish, looking down and seeing the whole world at once, seeing all the people getting into cars and washing dishes and feeding babies; seeing all the kids working on computers and doing their homework and watching TV; seeing all the teachers in their houses, grading assignments and drinking coffee; and seeing all the hamsters, too, running around in their cages and the fish swimming in their tanks; and even seeing a real skunk creeping around in the woods and a thief creeping around on the street; and there in the middle was a boy, fully dressed, in his bathtub, writing and worrying, alone.

CHAPTER SEVEN

The next morning Edgar kept his fingers crossed the entire bus ride and all the way down the hall. When he walked into Ms. Herschel's room and saw Mister Furball running on the wheel inside his cage, he uncrossed his fingers and slumped into his chair. No criminal had crept in. No thrilling second theft had occurred. It was just another ordinary day.

> I am disappointed that Mister Furball is safe. What kind of person am I?
>
> Ms. Herschel is about to take attendance, and Patrick Chen is still not here and all I'm thinking is I hope he is sick. How will I feel if Patrick Chen has a brain seizure and dies? Will I feel happy then? I am definitely not a nice person.

Just as Ms. Herschel was finishing taking the roll, Patrick walked in and announced that he had solved the mystery.

Edgar felt sick to his stomach. A metaphor poem came to him all at once. He grabbed his pencil.

ME
    by Edgar Allan
I am a big glass
but instead of being filled
with orange juice,
I am filled
with hatred.
Toward a certain someone.
Even though I know that isn't nice.

Ms. Herschel set down her coffee cup. "You've solved the crime already, Patrick?"

"Through interviews and forensic analysis," Patrick nodded.

Interviews and forensic analysis! All I have to rely on is my own stupid brain, Edgar thought.

"Yesterday I interviewed the principal and Mrs. Peabody at the front desk," Patrick went on. "They said there were no strangers on school property yesterday during the time of the crime, so I believe that the thief is someone who belongs at this school."

"Good job, Patrick!" Ms. Herschel said. "Interviewing is a great way to get information."

"Thank you! There's more!" Patrick held up a photo that he had printed out. "This is a shoe print. Someone with dirty shoes left this print right here at the scene of the crime." He pointed to the floor in front of the chalkboard. "As you can see, they don't belong to Ms. Herschel. I checked with Mr. Browning, the custodian. He said he mopped the floor the night before and did not return to the classroom in the morning. So...I believe the shoe prints belong to the thief." He pointed to the picture. "See this distinctive tread pattern with an "O" in the center? During recess, I found matching footprints in the mud. Through careful observation, I discovered who the footprints belong to."

Everyone was silent, waiting.

Patrick grinned.

"Well, who is it?" Kip blurted out.

"The person who has a shoe print with an 'O' is...Taz Raskel!"

"I knew it!" Maia exclaimed.

Everybody looked at Taz's feet.

"So? My shoe prints were on the floor," Taz argued. "What does that mean? I was the first person in the room. Of course my shoe prints would be on the floor."

"According to Ms. Peabody in the office, you were the first student in the *building*," Patrick said. "You had the time to commit the crime without being seen."

"Now Patrick," Ms. Herschel interrupted. "I like that you're observing shoe print impressions. That's what an investigator would look for. But remember, just because you find a shoe print near a crime scene, doesn't mean the shoe print belongs to the criminal. Taz does come in early every day to check on the pets, so it makes sense that his shoe prints would be here."

"Well," Patrick said, "I have another piece of evidence!" He held up another photograph.

"What is it?" Kip asked, trying to see.

"It's a photograph I took of a poem written in the boy's bathroom." Patrick read:

There once was a
great dude named Taz
who had a lot of
pizazz!
He likes to play jokes
on all kinds of folks
especially the kids in
his clazz!

Ms. Herschel looked at the picture and sighed. "Taz, that's your handwriting. You know you're not supposed to write on bathroom doors!"

"The poem proves that Taz likes to play jokes on people and likes poetry." Patrick summed it up. "Those are two things that are true of the thief. And we know that Taz is a pet lover. So my theory is that Taz wanted Slurpy all to himself. He took Slurpy, but then he felt guilty about it, so he called his mom. I was a witness."

"Wait!" Taz said. "Another crime has been committed. Someone stole the brain right out of Patrick's head."

The class laughed, but Patrick's theory made Taz look awfully guilty. Edgar couldn't bear the thought that Patrick had solved the crime, so he looked at the picture of Taz's poem, trying to find a hole in his theory. "Wait!" he cried. "Taz couldn't be the thief! The thief has great handwriting and Taz's is terrible!"

"Hey, he's right," Taz said.

Ms. Herschel nodded. "Interesting observation, Edgar. Forensic investigators often use handwriting analysis to solve crimes. Patrick...we can't accuse unless we have solid evidence. At this point, I believe we all still need to keep our eyes and ears open."

"Yeah, Patrick," Taz said.

Patrick glared at Edgar.

Ms. Herschel stepped between them. "Edgar, have you uncovered anything else that might help?"

Edgar looked at his notebook. Sadly, nothing he had done so far was any good. The theory about a professional fish thief, the worry about Mister Furball and the kindergarten fish...none of it had led him any closer to solving the crime. He shook his head.

"Well. I suggest we all keep our minds open," Ms. Herschel said. "Use your powers of observation. Consider all the possibilities. Remember the culprit is sometimes the opposite of who you'd expect."

I am going to try opening my mind
right now. Think...think...think...
    It could be anyone....Someone
who looks sweet on the outside
might be rotten on the inside. Like
an Easter bunny with rabies. Or
Clarice Stolnup!

The crime happened between 8:25 and 8:55 and no strangers were in the building. If the thief is someone from school, it can't be any of the kids on my bus because we didn't get there until 9:00. So...it must be a walker.

The walkers in my class are:

Kip, Taz, Patrick, Destiny, Maia, and Gabriela.

Kip is fast, and he wrote a really good poem. Could he have done it? Maybe he skateboarded in? No shoe prints then! But...he has even worse handwriting.

Aha! The doors of my mind just banged right open. Who is the opposite of a criminal? Destiny Perkins! She is the best student in the class, and the nicest, happiest girl. She never gets into trouble even when we have a substitute. She also has excellent handwriting and loves poetry.

One problem. She and Maia Gomez have been best friends since the first grade. Why would one best friend steal the goldfish that the other best friend gave to the class?

I am going to observe Destiny. Never fear! I will solve this mystery.

CHAPTER EIGHT

Destiny Perkins could hide a whole school of fish in her hair. Why hadn't Edgar noticed this before? It was shiny and wavy on top of her head where it was gathered together by a ponytail holder, and then it puffed out in a frizz of black curls.

Destiny was sitting two seats up and one row over, and even though Edgar knew she wasn't hiding fish in her hair, he wanted to use his powers of observation to notice everything about her.

He kept an eye on her all through math class, which meant that he didn't complete the sixteen problems that were due by the end of the period and so he had homework. It would have been worth it if he had uncovered a piece of damaging evidence, but all Destiny did the entire time was math. Math! He was beginning to have his doubts about her as a suspect.

On the way to Mr. Crew's room, the situation improved. Destiny walked alone, which was very suspicious. Destiny always walked with Maia.

Something is up between Destiny and Maia. Perhaps Maia knows that her best friend is a criminal and she has decided to no longer walk with her.

In language arts, Edgar finally had his chance to do some professional sleuthing. It all began with another poetry lesson.

Mr. Crew wrote a poem on the board.

What Am I?
Sometimes I am white.
Sometimes I am gray.
Sometimes I steal the sunlight.
Sometimes I float away.

The tall, lanky teacher finished writing, sat on the edge of his desk, and picked up his teacup. "What is the poem about? What am I?" he asked.

Patrick was the first one to raise his hand. "A cloud," he said.

Edgar knew the right answer. He would have said it, too, if only he could've raised his hand faster.

Note: The shirt I'm wearing is too small, which makes it hard for me to raise my arm. This is a problem because all my shirts are too small and my parents are too cheap to

buy me new ones. What I really
need are new parents.

Mr. Crew set down his cup. "A poem is a mystery to solve. As we discovered yesterday, the writer gives you clues and you have to figure out the poem's meaning. I want everybody to try writing a riddle poem like the cloud poem I wrote on the board. It doesn't have to rhyme, but don't reveal exactly what the poem is about...we'll try to guess what each poem is about when we read them out loud. Let's have a minute of silence to let our imaginations get to work."

Edgar picked up his pencil. He liked the idea that a poem is a mystery and he wanted to try writing a very mysterious one, but he had to observe Destiny for suspicious behavior.

Patrick was sitting next to him on the right, so he had to be very careful not to let him see who he was observing.

Destiny was staring at her blank page, which was odd. She usually started on assignments right away.

Why isn't Destiny writing? Is
she racked with guilt? Is she trying
to come up with a new crime?
I should be writing my own
poem, but it is hard to write your
own poem if you are spying.
I bet Patrick will be the first
person to raise his hand and read
his poem.

> I think Destiny just had a brain-
> storm because she is writing fast
> now and pressing down very hard
> on her pencil.

Edgar stared closely as Destiny's pencil worked its way across the page. Then, he had a brainstorm of his own. He picked up his pencil and a poem poured out.

What Am I?
> by Edgar Allan
> I am your thin friend.
> Pass your thoughts to me
> and I'll scratch them down
> for all to see,
> giving a bit of myself
> unselfishly
> for you.

He had never written anything like it. He read it over to make sure it was good. It *was* good. He liked the metaphor of the pencil as a friend. He imagined this pencil, loyal and brave, getting smaller and smaller with each use, in order to serve the writer. He liked the fact that his poem said all this without actually saying the word pencil at all.

He smiled at the pencil in his hand. Thank you, friend, he thought! He put his pencil down and raised his hand. His heart was pounding.

"Yes, Edgar?"

"I'm done!"

"Oh! Well, hold on. When everybody else is finished, you can go first."

A strange feeling was building inside Edgar, an excitement of a different kind. This was the third poem that he had written since Mr. Crew had started this poetry unit, and writing each one had been surprisingly satisfying. The thought that he might have a special talent for writing poems as well as for investigating mysteries occurred to him for the first time in his life.

He noticed Patrick looking in his direction. Edgar smiled at his nemesis, and then he raised his hand again.

"Yes, Edgar?"

"I'm done."

"Yes, I know. Just wait a few minutes longer, and you can read your poem for us."

Finally, the class was ready. But somehow Mr. Crew forgot that he had promised Edgar could go first, and Patrick was the first to raise his hand.

Patrick read:

What Am I?
I am your long skinny friend.
Give me your ideas.
When I scribble them down,
heads will bend to read them.

Edgar could hardly breathe.

"You're a pencil!" Maia said.

"Yep." Patrick nodded.

"It's a masterpiece!" Mr. Crew said. "I love the

metaphor of the pencil as a friend! Great job, Patrick! Who would like to go next? Edgar?"

"That was my...He..." Edgar looked at Patrick, but Patrick wouldn't look back. Patrick had stolen his idea! He had practically stolen the whole poem!

"Edgar, didn't you want to read yours?" Mr. Crew asked.

How could he read it now?

"We'll go!" Maia said.

Maia and Gabriela read another one that they wrote together, and Sammy read one about a soccer ball without enough air, and Taz read a funny one about the inside of a dog's nose, but Edgar couldn't pay attention.

> It is a terrible feeling to have something stolen from you. It's like you're about to eat a delicious feast and somebody comes along and pulls all the food away.
>
> Maybe a thief is somebody who has never had anything stolen because once you've had something stolen, then you know how bad it feels, and how could you ever do that to somebody else?

Toward the end of class, Edgar realized that he was neglecting his crime investigation duties. Come to think of it, something very odd *had* happened regarding Destiny during class. Destiny hadn't shared her poem. She always wanted to share. So, why not this time?

There were five minutes of class left, and they were supposed to be quietly brainstorming ideas for more poems on a page in their notebooks. Mr. Crew was busy putting up the poems from yesterday on his bulletin board.

Edgar decided to blow his nose. As he passed by Destiny's desk on his way to get a tissue, he peeked at the poem in her notebook. He walked as slowly as possible, but he could only read the first line. He grabbed a tissue, went back to his seat, blew his nose, and wrote down the first line of her poem. He had to go back four times in order to write it all down. And it was lucky he finished because Mr. Crew told him no more tissues.

What Am I?
by Destiny Perkins
I weep.
My graceful arms hang with the weight
of sadness.
Once I heard happy voices beneath me.
Now...silence.

Edgar read the poem five times. What did it mean? Mr. Crew was right. Poems are like mysteries that must be cracked open in order to be understood. He would have to think about this one for a while.

Before the bell rang, he needed to finish a new riddle poem, since Patrick had stolen his pencil poem. He rubbed his nose, which was sore from all the nose blowing, and wished he could think of a funny one like Taz. An idea came to him.

What Am I?
by Edgar Allan
Sometimes I run
Sometimes I'm stuffed
Sometimes one tissue
Is not enough.
I deliver all smells
From sour to sweet
Just don't ask me
To smell your feet.

Edgar held it up and read it over to himself. He liked it!
Behind him, Taz laughed. "Hey, let me see that!"
Edgar handed him the notebook.

GREAT poem, DUDE!

For once Edgar didn't mind that Taz had written in his notebook.

CHAPTER NINE

Teriyaki meatballs, salad, sliced peaches, milk, and a cookie. Edgar hardly paid attention to what he was carrying on his lunch tray. Destiny was ahead of him, sitting down at a crowded table. He wanted to sit close enough to overhear any important conversations, and there was only one spot left at her table. As he walked toward it, he noticed Sammy and Kip were headed in the same direction. Edgar walked faster, not noticing the sliced peach that was on the floor in his path. *Sloosh!* His foot hit it and he slipped and fell. Meatballs rolled, salad somersaulted, peaches plummeted, milk spilled, and the cookie crumbled.

"Way to go, Edgar!" Clarice Stolnup shouted out.

Mr. Browning gave Clarice a look that made her close her mouth. Then the nice custodian helped Edgar clean up.

Lunch was almost over by the time Edgar finally sat down with a new tray too far from Destiny's table to hear a thing. Oh well, recess would be the perfect time to spy on her, he thought. But just as he was taking a bite out of his cookie, Ms. Cassatt stopped by to remind him to come to the art room and finish painting his mask. Of all the rotten luck.

He gulped the rest of his lunch, ran to the art room, and began to paint his mask bright blue. While he was there, Ms. Barrett came in, her pretty face flushed and nervous. She pulled a stool over to Ms. Cassatt's desk, and Edgar couldn't help overhearing their hushed conversation.

"Did you give him the card?" Ms. Cassatt asked.

"Yes! But he hasn't said anything all day. I'm so embarrassed."

"Maybe he just didn't get it."

"I slipped it under the door of his supply closet yesterday. He had to have seen it."

"Maybe he's waiting for the right moment. What did you write in it?"

"A poem," Ms. Barrett whispered.

"Oh, that's so romantic! He loves poetry! He's always reading poetry."

"I know!"

Edgar began putting white and black and red dots on his mask. It was odd to hear teachers talking like this. It sounded like Ms. Barrett was in love! Edgar wondered who they were talking about.

Ms. Cassatt jumped. "There he is! Ask him!"

Edgar looked out the door and saw Mr. Browning walking by with a ladder.

Ms. Barrett pulled the other teacher back. *"Shh!"*

Edgar got out his notebook.

Ms. Barrett wrote a love poem
on a card and left it in Mr. Brown-

*ing's supply closet! Ms. Barrett has
a secret side. Does every teacher?*

He put the last spot of paint on his mask. The shape of the mask was his face, but the colors and designs made the mask look bold and powerful. Is this the real me or am I a boring, ordinary boy? he wondered. He washed his brushes and asked if he could go.

Finding Destiny was easy. She was where she always was during recess: sitting underneath the willow tree on the far end of the playground. But the picture was incomplete. Maia was usually with her. Where was Maia? She wasn't on the basketball court or by the giant chessboard or with Sammy and the other kids playing soccer in the field. He walked to the side of the building and peeked around the corner. Maia and Gabriela were there! Why were they hiding?

Edgar wondered if he had his theory backward: Maybe Destiny was staying away from Maia because she had become a thief with Gabriela!

"Let's start at the beginning again," Maia said.

The two girls stood back to back.

"*Uno, dos, tres, cuatro,*" Gabriela said, and then they began to dance.

Dance? What kind of thieves danced? Edgar stepped out from his hiding place. Maia stopped and made a face. "This is a *private* rehearsal."

"For what?"

"You know how Gabriela is the Star of the Month?" Maia asked.

Edgar knew. *He* had hoped to be chosen.

"Well," Maia continued. "She wanted to do a Mexican folk dance for her Star-of-the-Month talent, and I said I do Mexican folk dancing, and so she asked me if I would do a dance with her."

Gabriela smiled and nodded.

"Go away so we can practice," Maia said.

Edgar walked back to the main playground and sat on the tree stump. Back to investigating Destiny. He glanced at the willow tree, where Destiny was still sitting, and read over her poem again.

What Am I?
by Destiny Perkins
I weep.
My graceful arms hang
with the weight of sadness.
Once I heard happy voices
beneath me.
Now...silence.

An idea hit him like a ray of sunlight.

I think I cracked the mystery of Destiny's riddle poem. The answer is <u>willow tree!</u> The willow tree has graceful arms that hang down and it's weeping because Destiny and Maia used to sit beneath it and talk happily, and now there is only silence. Why is there only silence? Because Destiny is alone!

Maia and Destiny have been best friends since first grade. Now Maia isn't hanging out with Destiny anymore. I think Gabriela came along and stole Destiny's best friend! I think Destiny is sad and lonely!

Can sadness be a motive for stealing something? Or maybe she is jealous?

Did she steal the goldfish to get revenge on Maia for leaving her in the dust? Has she decided to turn to a life of crime?

Patrick is watching me! I cannot give away the fact that Destiny is my prime suspect. I will pretend to be observing somebody else.

I was pretending to observe Kip who was sitting on the bottom of the slide, eating a candy bar, and then Clarice Stolnup came along and stole the candy right out of Kip's hand. Kip got up to chase after her, but his shoe was untied and he tripped. Guess who went after Clarice and got the candy back for Kip?

Taz!

Life is a surprise.

CHAPTER TEN

Edgar was on a roll! After recess was over, it was time for social studies in Mr. Crew's room, and Edgar knew what he wanted to investigate: the metaphor poems from yesterday that were on the bulletin board. He hurried to class and searched until he found Destiny's.

Friend
by Destiny Perkins
A true friend swims
close to you
never leaving you
all alone
in the dirty water
of life.

Edgar understood it! She wasn't really talking about a fish. She was talking about her former best friend. Maia was the fish who swam away to be with Gabriela!

"Have a seat, class," Mr. Crew called out.

Edgar sat down. Destiny came in a moment later,

hugging her notebook to her chest, and quietly took her seat.

> Now that I have read Destiny's poems, I know more about her. She is sad, sad, sad.
>
> Is everybody hiding some kind of sad secret inside them? I guess some people have sadness in them and some people don't. I bet Taz is always in a good mood because he is always cracking jokes. I bet Patrick is never sad, either, because he is always succeeding in everything he does. They have it easy. Like my brother.

As Mr. Crew began his lesson on Mexico's history, Edgar began to reconstruct the crime from Destiny's point of view. On that fateful morning, she must have arrived early and found Ms. Herschel's classroom empty. She sat down, feeling miserable. Perhaps she looked over at Slurpy and recalled that her former best friend, Maia Gomez, had given the goldfish to the class as a gift. Angry, she wrote the poetic note, taped it to the board, and picked up Slurpy... but how? Did she put the fish in a bowl? And then what? If she left the classroom, certainly someone would have seen her walking around with a goldfish: Edgar's brown eyes grew bigger. She must have hid it in Ms. Hershel's room. But where? Maybe, just maybe, the fish was in Destiny's cubby!

He jumped up.

"What is it, Edgar?"

"I need to use the bathroom."

"You just got back from recess, Edgar. You can go after class. Have a seat."

"I have to use the bathroom, too," Sammy said.

"No bathroom breaks now," Mr. Crew said.

The lesson on Aztec trade and transportation went in one ear and out the other. Edgar simply could not concentrate. Today was PE, so after social studies, they went straight to the gym, which was on the opposite side of the school.

Finally, PE was over and they were heading back to Ms. Herschel's room for end-of-day dismissal. Edgar walked as fast as he possibly could. He wanted to be the first one there so he could look in Destiny's cubby and discover the goldfish!

Ms. Herschel was sitting at her desk grading papers when he rushed in.

"How was PE?" she asked.

"Fine!" Edgar zoomed straight to the back of the room. He found Destiny's cubby. In it was a pink jacket, a purple book bag, and a small twig with two graceful willow leaves.

No Slurpy.

"What are you looking at?" Patrick's voice made Edgar jump.

"Nothing!" Edgar said and rushed to his own cubby.

Patrick peered into Destiny's cubby.

"What are you looking at?" Destiny's voice made Patrick jump.

"Nothing!" Patrick said and glared at Edgar. "You don't know what you're doing, Edgar. I don't know why I'm bothering to keep my eye on you."

It's true. I don't know what I'm doing. If I were a butterfly, my wings would be torn. If I were a number, I'd be zero.

CHAPTER ELEVEN

That evening after dinner, Henri got out his clarinet and announced that he needed an audience. "Mr. Copland said we should practice all the songs for the fall band concert like it's the real deal."

"A man after my own heart," Tubby said, picking Rosy up out of her high chair. "A dress rehearsal tonight, Rosy! And we get to be the audience!"

For the occasion, Twig tried to put a little tiara head-band on Rosy, but Rosy made Tubby wear it on his bald head. Tubby placed a small top hat on top of Twig's red hair and asked, "What do you want to wear, Edgar?"

"I have homework," Edgar said.

His parents set up three chairs in the living room, and Tubby sat down in one with Rosy on his lap.

"Edgar, hurry, there's one seat left in the front row," Twig said. "You can do your homework later."

Standing in the doorway between the living room and the dining room, Edgar snapped. "I don't see the point. We've already listened to these songs a billion times."

It is one thing to get a disappointed look from an ordinary

mother, but a disappointed look coming from a woman who spends her days cheering up sick children is much worse.

"It's okay," Henri said. "I don't want him to stay if he's just going to be negative."

Edgar took his notebook and sat on the concrete steps outside the front door.

My parents think I'm being mean to Henri right now, but they don't see what's going on inside of me. I think I will explode if I have to sit there and watch Henri doing something good. Watching other people succeed is the story of my life.

Maybe I should tell them what I'm going through and explain how worried I am that Patrick will solve the crime before I do. But what if they don't think it's a serious problem?

It's funny how the outside of a person doesn't always match the inside.

Everybody thinks Destiny is happy. But she's not. Everybody thinks Taz just jokes around all the time. But he worries about butterflies. I hope neither of them committed the crime. I am still hoping it's the work of a professional thief.

Edgar stopped writing and looked up. The sun was setting behind the big magnolia tree in his neighbor's yard.

> The sky is the color of ten thousand goldfish. What if the reds and oranges and golds of the setting sun were caused by the last rays of light bouncing off all the goldfish spirits flying around in heaven?
>
> Who knows what really happens to fish or to people or to butterflies after they die? Maybe everything has a spirit and every spirit has a color and it just can't be seen all the time.

Edgar's neighbor Mr. Timmid was out, raking leaves. He stopped and leaned on his rake and looked at the sky, just like Edgar was doing. Edgar's heart squeezed. He remembered when Mr. Timmid's wife had died. Edgar was a second grader at the time and it was the only funeral he had ever been to.

> Is Mr. Timmid thinking about his wife's spirit? Is he missing her with all his might? He must be lonely. I sort of forgot about her, which makes me feel bad. I wonder how many people, at this very moment in time, are sad? I wonder how many people are looking up at the sky?

CHAPTER TWELVE

Overnight, dark thunderclouds had invaded, and now the rain was pounding on top of the school bus like it was trying to get in. An ominous morning. As the bus pulled into the school parking lot, Edgar peered out to see if any criminal-looking types were lurking around the school's entrance.

The car ahead of them pulled up to the curb, and Destiny hopped out, running so she wouldn't get wet. She and Maia weren't even carpooling in the rain together, Edgar noticed. He wondered if Destiny's parents knew that she had lost her best friend in the world. Or was she hiding it from them, too?

As he got out of the bus, Edgar tried to think of something nice he could say to cheer her up, but his mind was blank.

"Good morning!" Mr. Browning said as he walked by with his broom.

Edgar said good morning and then thought about Ms. Barrett. Had Mr. Browning said anything to her about the card she gave to him? Did he love her back?

When Edgar turned the corner, he saw Ms. Barrett with a frown on her face. Maybe if she smiled more, Mr. Browning would like her. But then again, maybe the reason she wasn't smiling was because he didn't love her in return! It was all very confusing.

When Edgar arrived at his classroom, Kip was guarding the door. "Patrick says you can come in, but nobody can touch anything," he said.

"Another crime has been committed!" Patrick said importantly. He was at the board, where another note was taped, measuring the distance from the floor to the note.

Edgar kicked himself for not getting there earlier. Why couldn't he have been the one to find the note?

"What was stolen?" Destiny asked.

"Come in and have a seat, everybody," Ms. Herschel said. "The beautiful silk iris—the flower—that I had in my pencil cup is gone. Mr. Crew gave me that last Christmas." She read the note again for all the newcomers.

Stopping by This Room on a Rainy Morning

Whose room this is I think I know
I'm glad to find it empty so
No eyes will see me stopping here
To pluck the bloom and go.

"To pluck the bloom" was a clever way of saying "to steal the flower," Edgar thought. The thief certainly was poetic! Ms. Herschel had said it was an iris. Maybe that was important. He whipped out his notebook.

> An iris was stolen! I wasn't
> expecting this. Why an iris?
> Think...think...think...

"When did it happen, Ms. Herschel?" Maia asked.

"The flower was here when I first arrived. Then, it happened the same way...I left the room to get coffee, and when I came back it was gone," Ms. Herschel said.

> Coffee again! When will this
> woman learn?

Patrick put away his tape measure and turned to face the class triumphantly. "I've just verified my theory! The thief taped the note in approximately the same place he did last time."

"What does that mean?" Kip asked.

"See how I have to reach to touch it? Well, that means the thief is probably taller than average."

Everybody looked at Taz.

Taz laughed. "What would I want with a flower?"

"And look!" Patrick said, crouching down and pointing to the floor. "More shoe prints with an 'O'."

"That doesn't mean anything," Taz argued. "Your shoe prints are there, too, Patrick. I got here first, and when I saw the note, I went to find Ms. Herschel."

Edgar looked at the new message. "Like I said before, Taz couldn't write that good if he tried!"

Patrick smirked and handed Ms. Herschel her measuring tape. "Can I tell about the handwriting analysis I did?"

"I already analyzed!" Edgar said. "Anybody could see it's not his!"

"I did some *real* handwriting analysis." Patrick smiled. "Yesterday after school, I looked carefully at the first note the way a real forensic investigator would. I looked at connecting strokes, and line quality, and spacing of words and letters, and pen pressure on both downward and upward strokes. And I realized that the handwriting looked *extremely* regular and the pressure on each letter looked *exactly* the same. I hypothesized that the note was printed by a computer with a font that looks like handwriting instead of being real handwriting! I checked the fonts that we have on our computers here at school, and it is an exact match for the font called "Frost Special."

"Wow! Great detective work, Patrick!" Ms. Herschel exclaimed.

"That's just the beginning," Patrick said. "I realized that I could use chromatography to determine exactly what brand of printer ink was used. You see, ink isn't just one color. It looks black, but really it's a mix of different colors. Each color has a different particle size. And if you dissolve the ink in a certain way you can see the particular spectrum of colors, which is sort of like the ink's signature. So I dissolved the ink and made this. It's called a chromatogram."

He held out the thief's first note. The ink had bled into a kind of rainbow of yellow, blue, red, and purple.

"That's chemistry, Patrick!" Ms. Herschel said.

"I know." Patrick smiled. "This morning before school, I did a chromatogram of the ink we use at this school, and it's a perfect match." He held up another chromatogram. "I checked with Mrs. Peabody and I found out that all the ink used by the school's printers is the same brand, and it's not a brand that people can order outside of the school system, which means that the notes *had* to be printed at school."

"Excellent work!" Ms. Herschel exclaimed.

"I'm not making an accusation yet, but since the thief used a computer to print the notes, I have proven that even somebody with sloppy handwriting could be the thief." Patrick looked pointedly at Edgar and then at Taz.

> Patrick has used fancy ways to figure out that the thief is tall and used the school computer to write the notes! Patrick's important scientific father is probably helping him. I hate him and all his fancy words and ways.
>
> I don't want to believe Taz did it. But I will have to keep my eye on him. Kip is also a suspect again, since the only reason I took him off the list was his handwriting.

"Patrick, you have done some nice detective work. Like I said, let's all keep an open mind," Ms. Herschel said.

Maia raised her hand. "Don't forget it's Star of the Month talent day!"

"That's right," Ms. Herschel said. "Our Star of the Month is Gabriela. Before we start our science lesson, Gabriela will have her moment to shine. Gabriela, are you ready?"

Gabriela and Maia hopped out of their seats and went to the front of the room. Maia explained why she was dancing with Gabriela and handed Ms. Herschel a CD, which Ms. Herschel popped into her computer. As soon as guitar music filled the room, the two girls faced each other and began to dance.

Edgar's mind was racing. Why didn't he think of measuring how high on the board the note was taped?

Wait! The thief doesn't have to be tall. It could be someone short who is standing on something or jumping. What about Kip? He could use his skateboard to stand on. I bet Patrick didn't think of that! Kip could have done it before anyone saw him.

Or maybe it's Clarice Stolnup and she stood on a chair! I should keep my eye on her, but it's too hard since she's not in my classes. For sure, I'll keep an eye on Taz and Kip.

Why oh why are we born with only two eyeballs anyway?

In a snap, he realized one thing: Destiny could not have committed the crime. Edgar had seen her getting out of her mom's car after the crime had already been committed.

He looked at her. She was sitting perfectly still, watching Maia and Gabriela dance.

Right now, I'm watching Destiny. It's like she is wearing a mask that looks happy on the outside, but I can tell she's crying on the inside because Maia is dancing with Gabriela.

I'm glad that Destiny is not the thief! Then she'd be a criminal on top of being sad, and being sad is enough for one person.

I guess I'm wearing a mask, too. Everybody who looks at me just sees this perfectly happy normal boy, but inside I am upset about how Patrick keeps beating me.

I will focus my attention now on Taz and Kip and see if I can uncover any clues. I have to rely on my own brain.

CHAPTER THIRTEEN

During math class, Edgar spied on Kip. Kip's leg was jiggling against his desk, but his leg always did that. He
turned his attention to Taz and noticed something suspicious. Taz was staring at something in his hand instead
of paying attention to the lesson. What was it? Something
else he stole? Edgar had to get a look.

Edgar made a silent apology to his friend the pencil,
and then he broke off the tip.

"Ms. Herschel?" He raised his hand. "May I sharpen
my pencil?"

"I saw you break it!" Patrick whispered. "What are
you doing?"

"None of your business," Edgar whispered back.

Patrick raised his hand. "I need to sharpen mine, too."

"Boys. I'm in the middle of a lesson! You may both
sharpen your pencils when I'm done."

Ms. Herschel went on with the lesson. As soon as it
was over and the assignment to begin work was given,
Edgar and Patrick both jumped up. Edgar raced to the
sharpener, purposefully *not* passing by Taz's desk. Patrick

followed him. Edgar was so mad, he couldn't hold his pencil straight, and he had to try three times to get it sharp.

"What are you doing?" Patrick whispered angrily.

"What are *you* doing?" Edgar whispered back.

On the way back to his desk, Edgar took a chance. He passed by Taz's desk and glanced over without moving his head so that Patrick couldn't see.

Taz was staring at a keychain!

Quickly, he slid into his seat and pretended to begin work on his math. Two seconds later Patrick leaned over and whispered, "I bet he stole that keychain, too!"

Edgar's pencil broke again.

Ms. Herschel set her coffee cup down and mouthed the words, "Get to work," at Edgar.

Edgar looked at her coffee cup and a fresh idea filled him to the brim. He grabbed his notebook and hurried to his teacher's desk.

OFFICIAL INTERVIEW
WITH MS. HERSCHEL

EDGAR: May I ask you a question?

MS. HERSCHEL: Is it about the division, multiplication, subtraction, or addition of fractions?

EDGAR: It is about the subtraction of an iris from this room.

MS. HERSCHEL: I thought so.

EDGAR: Who would you say
                   is the worst of
                   all your enemies,
                   ma'am?

MS. HERSCHEL: I don't really
                   have any enemies,
                   Edgar.

EDGAR: What about coffee?

MS. HERSCHEL: What about coffee?

EDGAR: Everyone knows
                   you drink a lot of
                   it, ma'am. Other
                   teachers might
                   want some cof-
                   fee, too. Per-
                   haps you are
                   known as a cof-
                   fee hog. Perhaps
                   another teacher
                   is stealing your
                   prized possessions
                   as revenge for the
                   fact that you hog
                   the coffee.

MS. HERSCHEL: Edgar, I believe
                   you are the first
                   person in the
                   entire world to call
                   me a coffee hog.

EDGAR: I would say it
                   takes one to know

one, ma'am, but I
don't like coffee.

MS. HERSCHEL: You're one of a
kind, Edgar.

EDGAR: Thank you. Do you
know what Mr.
Crew drinks?

MS. HERSCHEL: Tea.

EDGAR: Exactly.

MS. HERSCHEL: And what does
that have to do
with this?

EDGAR: He's never had
anything stolen
from his room,
has he?

MS. HERSCHEL No.

EDGAR: Maybe you should
switch.

IMPORTANT CONCLUSION:
   Ms. Herschel is finally seeing the
light.

Edgar closed his notebook and let his new theory percolate. Another teacher is stealing Ms. Herschel's possessions because Ms. Herschel is a coffee hog. An original theory, Edgar was sure. He watched the clock. He wanted to be first out the door, so that he could be the one to tell Mr. Crew about the latest theft.

CHAPTER FOURTEEN

Edgar was first out the door, with Patrick at his heels.

"Look! It's the thief!" Patrick yelled.

Edgar turned to look, and Patrick sped ahead, laughing.

By the time Edgar arrived at Mr. Crew's classroom, Patrick had already showed him the thief's message. When everyone was seated, the teacher asked Patrick to read it again to the entire class. "Listen to the meter as he reads it," Mr. Crew said. "Meter is the rhythm of the poem. Listen to how this poem sounds. 'Whose room this is I think I know.' *Ba bum, ba bum, ba bum, ba bum.*"

Patrick read the poem.

"Why do you think some poets use meter or rhythm?" Mr. Crew asked.

"Because they like hip hop," Taz said.

"Because it gives the poem a beat," Maia said.

"Yes! Any other ideas?"

"It's like a heartbeat," Destiny said.

"Yes! Rhythm is all around us and *in* us. The heartbeat is the first thing we hear, even before we're born! We hear our mother's heartbeat and it connects us. Everybody sit down and listen." He drummed a rhythm on his desk with the palms of his hands. "Come on, connect to the rhythm."

Taz was first. He started thumping the rhythm on his desk. Everyone else joined in. At first, Edgar didn't want to participate because he felt so cheated out of being first to the room, but the rhythm was like a voice, calling him to join in. When Edgar began drumming, he felt as if he had become a part of some big, living thing that was outside and inside himself at the same time.

As a group, they began to drum faster and louder, each student certain the principal was going to come in and tell them to stop.

"Boom! Boom! Boom!" Mr. Crew said to the beat.

"Booming in the room!" Taz yelled.

"Boom! Boom! Boom!" Mr. Crew chanted. "Booming in the room!"

They all started chanting. "Boom! Boom! Boom! Booming in the room!"

The beat began to slow down and get softer and softer and finally it came to a stop.

"Let's boom it again," Taz said.

Mr. Crew laughed. "If you read a poem with meter, the rhythm helps you to connect with the poem, with the message of the poem, and even with the poet. A poem is a connection. Everybody take a minute, and get silent. Try to hear a rhythm. Then try writing a poem with that rhythm."

Edgar sat very still and tried to get in touch with his inner rhythm. The silence was electrifying. His heart was thumping a mile a minute, probably because he was still mad at Patrick. *Ba bum, ba bum, ba bum, ba bum.* He looked around. Taz had his eyes closed. He wondered what he was thinking about. He looked at Destiny. She had her eyes closed, too.

The rain was still coming down, plunking against the windows with a rhythm of its own. Edgar watched the water streaming down in little rivers.

He looked at Destiny again. Even with her eyes closed, she looked sad to him. Would she look sad to anybody else? Or just him because he knew her secret sadness?

Edgar looked at the sentence Mr. Crew had painted above the board. "A poem is a gift." A remarkable idea occurred to Edgar. What if he left a poem in her cubby?...He took out a sheet of paper.

Stopping by Your Cubby on a Gray Day
It's raining now. I think I hear
Each droplet falling like a tear
I spy your pain and want to say
You're not alone! So never fear!

Careful not to let Patrick see, he folded the paper, wrote Destiny's name on it, and put it in his pocket. Now his heart was pounding louder than ever. Would he have the guts to follow through with it?

"Edgar, it looks like you're finished," Mr. Crew said. "Would you like to read yours?"

"No!" Edgar yelped.

"Destiny, how about you?" Mr. Crew asked.

Destiny looked down. "No, thanks."

Mr. Crew paused with a smile, waiting to see if either of them would change their minds. Then, he looked out at his class.

"What about you, Taz?"

Taz grinned. "Sure."

Edgar switched gears in his brain, away from thinking about Destiny back to Taz. Before he had come up with his new theory about a coffee-loving teacher taking revenge on Ms. Herschel, Taz was his prime suspect. Edgar had to follow through with the coffee lead, but also, he had to keep focused on his classmates.

Taz read his poem.

Fetch

I fling it far across the field.
My dog goes chasing after.
He grabs it in his slobberjaws
and runs back even faster.
Next time I play fetch with my dog,
a stick is what I'll use,
instead of mom's new oven mitt,
which now is wet and chewed.

Mr. Crew laughed. "Great poem, Taz! The rhythm of your poem matches the rhythm of your dog running back and forth! I almost feel like I'm there, playing fetch with him, too. And I love how you use alliteration in the first line. Who knows what I mean by that?"

Edgar couldn't think about alliteration at the moment. He was stuck on the fact that Taz had written another dog poem.

*Possible clue: Taz has written three
poems so far, and all three are
about his dog. A clue? Maybe not.
If my mom would let me get a dog,
I'd probably write a lot of great
poems.*

Since he wasn't about to turn in his poem about Destiny, Edgar had to write another rhythm poem to turn in to Mr. Crew.

Think...think...think...
Why can't I
think...think...think...
I think my
brain...brain...brain
is going to
shrink...shrink...shrink
It needs a
drink...drink...drink
of magic
ink...ink...ink
that drips with
rhyme...rhyme...rhyme
So I can
find...find...find
A poem in
time...time...time!

CHAPTER FIFTEEN

Secrets have a way of making the heart beat faster, and so Edgar's heart was galloping as he walked back to Ms. Herschel's room. He pulled his secret—the poem for Destiny—out of his pocket and slipped it onto the top shelf of her cubby.

"We're having indoor recess because of the rain, Edgar," Ms. Herschel called out. "What'll it be today? Would you like to sign out a game?"

Edgar popped out from behind the cubbies. "Can I sign up for computer #1?"

She nodded and he sat down at a computer in the back corner. From there, he could see the whole room at once. A perfect set-up for spying.

> Note: Ms. Herschel is at it again.
> Is her coffee cup ever empty? I
> don't think so.

Taz came in next. "I get computer #2!"

Ms. Herschel stopped him. "Last indoor recess

somebody set the alarm clock on the computer to play 'The Star Spangled Banner' during my afternoon class."

"That wasn't me!"

"I didn't say it was! I'm just reminding you and Edgar to use the computer appropriately."

Taz settled next to Edgar. The keychain he had been looking at earlier was hanging from his belt loop! Edgar tilted his head so he could get a better look. It was one of those keychains with a mini frame and in the frame was a picture of Taz's dog, Bandit, a German shepherd with a thick brown coat and black around his big brown eyes. Edgar recognized him right away. When Edgar and Taz were in the second grade, Bandit followed Taz to school. Taz couldn't get him to go home. Bandit trotted right beside him and sat next to Taz's desk. Everybody begged to let Bandit stay, but Mrs. Clint said no way. Taz's mom had to come and carry Bandit out, and he wimpered like he was really going to miss Taz. Edgar remembered going home that very day and asking his mom for a dog like Bandit.

So the keychain belonged to Taz; it wasn't stolen. He wondered if Patrick knew that.

Wait a minute! Taz's dog was named Bandit. Was that a clue or a coincidence? Was Taz training him to be a fellow criminal? Perhaps Edgar should be looking for paw prints rather than shoe prints!

Edgar looked back at his own computer, so Taz wouldn't catch him spying. He typed in the word "iris."

As he was scrolling through the various articles about irises that had popped up, more kids came into the room. A group followed Patrick over to his desk. Patrick was whispering about something, probably telling them more about chromatography, and then he called out to the teacher. "Ms. Herschel, can I take the note from the thief home and run fingerprint tests on it? My dad said he'd show me how to do it with a chemical solution called ninhydrin."

"That sounds like real forensic science, Patrick!" she said. "Be my guest."

Patrick looked at Edgar and smiled. Edgar did not smile back.

Girls came—Maia and Gabriela among them—and joined the group around Patrick's desk. Destiny walked in and headed straight for her cubby.

Edgar held his breath. Destiny's back was to him, so he couldn't see her face, but he knew by the way she was standing still that she had found the note and was reading it. She turned around, and Edgar quickly focused back on his screen.

Did she like it?

Edgar wanted to find out, but he didn't want to risk looking at her.

He forced his brain back to the crime…and to Taz.

So far all he was learning from the computer was that an iris grows from a bulb and takes its name from the Greek word meaning rainbow. Not very good clues.

Edgar glanced over at Taz's fingers on the computer keyboard.

Taz bites his fingernails! I thought I was the only one who did that. What does he have to be nervous about? Maybe he is the

> thief and he is nervous that I will
> find real evidence against him....

Edgar leaned back in his chair and pretended to yawn. If he tilted his head to the left, he could just see what was on Taz's screen.

Taz was reading an article:

What to Expect When Your Dog Has Osteosarcoma

Edgar froze. He didn't know what osteosarcoma was, but it didn't sound good. Taz was hunched forward, scrolling down through the article.

Quickly, Edgar turned his computer screen slightly away from Taz and typed in the question: **What is osteosarcoma?**

The answer came up: **Bone Cancer.**

Edgar stared at the words. Then he logged off. Quietly, he took his notebook and went to his desk.

> Does Bandit have cancer? If I was Taz's best friend, I'd ask him. Should I ask him even if I'm not his best friend? What if I ask him and it just makes him sad?
>
> Maybe Taz cracks jokes to cover up the fact that he is worried about Bandit. He must have a hard time concentrating in school. And on top of it, everybody thinks he is a thief!

Never fear, Taz! I will prove your innocence.

OFFICIAL INTERVIEW
WITH MR. CREW

EDGAR: Mr. Crew, which of the teachers at this school is the biggest coffee drinker, besides Ms. Herschel?

MR. CREW: That's an interesting question. Why do you ask?

EDGAR: I'm just doing my job, sir.

MR. CREW: Well, I know the staff lounge is usually full of coffee drinkers in the morning, but I brew my tea in my room, so I really don't know. I think Mr. Browning makes the coffee, but I'm not sure. You could ask him. You'd better go to class or you'll be late, Edgar.

IMPORTANT CONCLUSION:
Mr. Crew has gray hairs in his mustache if you look up close.

OFFICIAL INTERVIEW
WITH MR. BROWNING

EDGAR: Mr. Browning, do you or do you not make the coffee in the staff lounge?

MR. BROWNING: I do, Edgar. I'm usually the first one here, so I make a pot, grab a cup, and get to work. I need my coffee almost as much as Ms. Herschel!

EDGAR: Aha! So, the two of you are the biggest coffee drinkers?

MR. BROWNING: Well, she is first to the pot after me.

EDGAR: Thank you, Mr. Browning. I just have one more question for you. Do you know if Ms. Barrett drinks coffee?

MR. BROWNING: Ms. Barrett? Yes, she does. She takes cream and sugar.

EDGAR: Aha.

MR. BROWNING: Aha what?

EDGAR: Aha nothing. I have to go to class.

IMPORTANT CONCLUSIONS:

1. Ms. Herschel is a well-known coffee hog.
2. Mr. Browning is in love with Ms. Barrett. When I mentioned her name, this look came into his eyeballs.
3. If I ever fall in love, I'm wearing sunglasses so nobody can tell.

CHAPTER SIXTEEN

The rain had stopped, but the afternoon sun was still hiding behind the gray clouds, as if it knew there was more rain to come. As soon as Edgar arrived home, he put his crime investigation notebook in his backpack and hopped on his bike. Dodging the big puddles and driving slowly through the shallow ones, Edgar rode to Taz's street. Hopefully he'd see Taz and he could strike up a conversation. He could tell him that he didn't believe he was the thief—at least that might cheer him up.

As Edgar approached the house, he saw Taz and Bandit in their front yard. What luck! Bandit was peeing on a tree! Edgar pulled his bike behind the mail carrier's van and peeked out.

Everything was looking normal. Maybe Edgar had jumped to conclusions. But then Bandit stumbled. Edgar held his breath. Slowly, too slowly, the dog limped a few steps and sat down. After a few seconds, Bandit went down on his front paws, too. Taz stood, looking at him.

*I don't know much about dogs,
but I don't think they usually lie
down in wet grass.*

Edgar looked up. What Taz did next almost broke Edgar's heart. He sat next to his dog in the soaking grass. Gently, he stroked his fur and said something that Edgar couldn't hear.

Edgar didn't move a muscle.

After another minute, it began to drizzle lightly again. Taz stood up and called Bandit's name. Bandit turned his head to look at Taz, but he didn't get up.

Taz crouched down and tried to pick him up.

Edgar almost couldn't bear to watch. He wanted to help, but how could he?

Taz went inside and got his older brother. Together they lifted Bandit up and managed to carry him into the house.

Edgar gripped the handlebars of his bike, his face wet. He turned his bike around. And there, on her bike, was Destiny.

He could tell by the look in her eyes that she had witnessed the whole scene with Taz and Bandit.

"Bandit has cancer," she said. "He's dying."

Edgar stood, holding onto his bike in the drizzle. "I know. I saw Taz reading about it on the computer. How did you find out?"

"My mom is friends with Taz's mom," she explained.

They both looked at Taz's house. The hood of Destiny's red raincoat was up, her face serious and dark. "You left that poem in my cubby, didn't you," she said.

A little jolt ran through Edgar. "How did you know?" he asked.

"I recognized your handwriting."

He hadn't thought of that.

"Are you the thief?" she asked.

"*Me?* Why would you think that?"

"Because the thief leaves poems and because you always look suspicious and you write good poems, too."

Edgar felt himself blushing. "I thought *you* might be the thief."

"Me?" She smiled, one tooth missing on the side.

"I thought Taz might be the thief, too," Edgar said. "But I don't think so anymore."

"I don't think so either. Taz was upset when Slurpy disappeared, but he didn't want to show it." Destiny hesitated and looked again at Taz's house. "We should do something for him."

Edgar agreed. "I thought about telling him I think he's innocent. I thought that might make him feel better."

She parked her bike and pulled a notebook and pencil out of her backpack. "Let's write him a poem. We'll make it funny because Taz likes funny stuff. I write a line. You write a line," Destiny said. "We have to make it quick or it'll get too wet."

We know you're not the thief.
We know you're not the robber.
You're just like us, a normal kid,
Who likes to spit and slobber.

90

As soon as Edgar wrote the last line, he wanted to kick himself. It was stupid. Destiny wouldn't like the spit and slobber part. But she laughed. She ripped the page out of the notebook, folded it up, and handed it to him. "Quick. Put it in his mail slot."

"What if he hears me and looks out and sees us?"

She put her backpack on. "We'll make a getaway. I'll hold your bike so it's ready."

The mail slot was waiting. Edgar slipped the poem under his jacket to protect it from the rain, ran across the street, and popped it into the mail slot on Taz's door. When he came back, he hopped on his bike and they both began to pedal like crazy. Side by side they rode for a block on the wet pavement as fast as they could. Edgar was running out of breath, but he had never felt so good. He looked over and Destiny was smiling. She felt good, too.

They came to a fork in the road. Destiny lived to the right, and Edgar lived to the left.

Far off, the sky rumbled.

"See you tomorrow, Edgar," Destiny said.

"Yeah," Edgar said.

They each turned and rode home.

CHAPTER SEVENTEEN

When Edgar walked in the back door his mother yelped. "You're dripping wet, Edgar! Why didn't you come home as soon as it started to drizzle?"

"Because he left his brain in his cubby," Henri, proud owner of a middle-school locker, said as he poured himself a glass of milk.

Edgar smiled. "Mom, you should get Henri's eyes checked. He can't seem to see brilliance when it's standing right in front of him." He took the glass of milk that Henri had just poured, drank it, and said, "Thanks!"

Henri was speechless.

Dinner that night was his favorite. Tortellini tossed with olive oil and parmesan cheese. He ate every bite. Henri hogged the conversation again, but Edgar didn't care. Something had happened to him. Something big. He had written Destiny a poem that made her feel better. And together they had witnessed a profound and beautiful scene when they saw Taz try to care for Bandit with such love. Then they had written a poem to make him feel better, too. Mr. Crew was right. A poem was a gift.

After dinner, he took his notebook outside and sat on the concrete steps. The air was damp, but he didn't mind. The sky, dramatic and brooding, was folding over itself in different shades of gray. He wondered if Bandit was still alive and if Taz was watching over him.

I know that everything has to die, but sometimes I wonder why it has to be that way? Why can't it be that everything lives a really long time? Like hundreds of years? Perhaps I will be a doctor in addition to being a detective, and then I can find a cure for cancer.

I just looked at my own hand holding this pencil, and I thought, some day I'm going to die and then this hand will turn to bones.

I think there's something in me that's stronger than bones. My spirit. I don't think it has any one place in my body where it lives. I think it swirls and floats and zips around inside me. It's the moving part of me, the part of me that _feels_. When something really big is happening—either in a sad way or in a joyful way—I think my spirit expands and fills up my whole body. That happened today in a sad way when I saw Taz with Bandit and

again in a happy way when Destiny
and I left that poem for him. When
we were riding our bikes together,
my spirit was filling up my whole
body. Even the puddles looked like
works of art.
    Destiny could feel it, too. Eye-
balls never lie.

Edgar pulled out his notebook. He closed his eyes and let a great silence wash over him. Then he opened his eyes and wrote a poem. He read it over to himself. He crossed out a few words and chose better words. He read it again. Satisfied, he took his notebook into the living room. His parents were sitting on the floor, practicing a new card trick. Rosy was jumping up and down in her special Baby Bouncer harness that was attached to the doorjamb.

"I just wrote a poem," he said.

They looked up.

"Do you want to hear it?" he asked.

"Sure. Let 'er rip," his dad said.

Edgar read.

<u>**Inside**</u>
    by Edgar Allan
There is a you
inside you
stronger than bone
lighter than wind.
It shines like sunlight

through green magnolia leaves.
Ride through the rain,
it whispers.
Don't be afraid,
it whispers.
If a friend needs you,
sit down next to him
even if the grass
is wet.

His parents were silent. Then his mother smiled, her eyes brimming. "Wow, Edgar."

"Wow indeed," his dad said. "That was beautiful."

Even Rosy had stopped bouncing and was looking up at him, her toes just touching the floor, her big eyes filled with wonder.

"Thank you." Edgar took his notebook with him into the kitchen and helped himself to an extra large bowl of ice cream with whipped cream on top.

CHAPTER EIGHTEEN

The next morning on his way to the bus stop, Edgar saved three worms from drying out by picking them up and putting them back in the wet grass. The bus was late, so he had time for a quick entry.

> Maybe the reason people have pets is because it feels good to take care of something even if you know it might die someday. The good weighs more than the sad.
> Perhaps if my parents knew that I was saving worms, they would finally buy me a dog.

On the ride to school, the wheels of his mind turned faster than the wheels of the bus. Today was Friday. What would the day bring? Another crime? More interesting conversations with Destiny? A clue from Taz that he had received their poem and that it had cheered him up?

When his bus pulled up, Destiny was standing by the

flagpole. As soon as Edgar got off the bus, she walked over.

"Do you think the thief struck again?" she asked.

"I was just wondering about that," Edgar said.

"Great minds think alike," she said, and they walked in.

Even though Edgar and Destiny had gone to school together since kindergarten, they had never walked down the hall like this, side by side, until today. It felt a little odd. But in a good way, Edgar thought.

When they arrived at the classroom door, all the kids were standing outside it.

"It's locked!" Patrick said.

"I was the first one here," Kip said.

Just then Ms. Herschel walked up with a cup of coffee in one hand and a stack of books in the other.

Mr. Crew stepped out of his room at the same time. "Ah, the huddled masses yearning to breathe free have arrived!"

"I locked my door, Mr. Crew," Ms. Herschel said. "There's a thief running around."

"So I've heard," Mr. Crew said. "We've been studying the thief's poetry. Any break in the case?"

"Well, this locked door should keep everything safe." Ms. Herschel shifted the books in her hand. "Mr. Crew, can you do me a favor and open up for me?"

Mr. Crew unlocked her door and held it open.

Patrick squeezed in ahead of everyone else. "Another note!" he squealed.

"No way!" Ms. Herschel exclaimed.

Edgar and Destiny ran to the board, looked at the

note, and then exchanged excited glances. The students crowded around with Ms. Herschel and Mr. Crew.

Patrick read the note out loud.

I'm the Thief! Who are you?

I'm the Thief! Who are you?
Are you—a thief—too?
I have a secret. Ssh!—don't tell
Until you know for certain.

How dreary to be someone dull
So I made this plan
To take a risk, to sneak and steal
Ms. Herschel's fancy fan!

"My fan?" Ms. Herschel looked at the empty spot on the top of her bookshelf where a beautiful red and black lace fan was usually displayed along with other gifts she had received from past students.

"Not your Spanish fan!" Mr. Crew exclaimed. "Didn't a student give that to you?"

"Yes! It was right here—do you all remember it?"

Edgar did. He enjoyed looking at all the knickknacks Ms. Herschel kept on her shelf.

"This is getting serious!" Mr. Crew said. "I'd better go back and check my room."

"I could skateboard around the neighborhood," Kip

offered. "And if I see somebody with a fan I could chase him down."

"I think you'd better stay in the classroom, Kip," Ms. Herschel said. "Patrick, did your fingerprint test on the last note turn up anything?"

"No," Patrick said. "My dad said it was contaminated with too many prints. Nobody touch this one!"

"He's right," Ms. Herschel said.

She handed him an envelope for him to put it in. With a great flourish he pulled a tissue out of her box and used it to keep his own fingerprints off the message as he tucked it into the envelope.

"Everyone have a seat," Ms. Herschel said.

"Maybe you should call the police," Maia suggested.

Ms. Herschel sighed. "I was hoping that one of you would solve this mystery so that we wouldn't have to bring in the police, but maybe you're right."

Edgar and Destiny exchanged glances again.

> Destiny is excited that something else got stolen, too. She wants to solve this mystery with me!

Taz walked in and handed Ms. Herschel a note from his mom and noticed that something was going on. "What's up?" he asked.

"My fan from Spain was stolen," Ms. Herschel said. "Have a seat."

As Taz walked to his seat, he looked first at Edgar and then at Destiny.

*He got the note and knows
we wrote it! I can tell! And he's
excited there was another crime,
too! Isn't it amazing how much eyeballs can say?*

"Where have you been?" Patrick whispered to Taz.
"None of your business," Taz said.

Edgar was dying to ask Taz the same thing and to find out if Bandit was feeling better. He also thought that maybe Taz and Destiny would be interested in his theory about Ms. Herschel being a coffee hog and the thief being another teacher who was taking revenge, but Ms. Herschel interrupted his thoughts by beginning the day's lesson.

*I could get a lot more done in
school if there wasn't so much
school work to do.*

CHAPTER NINETEEN

"So where were you between 8:20 and 9:00, Taz?" Patrick glued himself to Taz's side as the class walked from math to language arts.

"At the dentist," Taz said.

Edgar chimed in. "So that means Taz couldn't have committed the crime, Patrick. Your theory is blown."

Patrick threw him a look. "He *says* he was at the dentist."

"Smell my strawberry-flavored fluoride!" Taz breathed on Patrick.

Edgar laughed.

Mr. Crew was waiting at his door. "Any more clues or evidence?"

"I'm working on it," Patrick said.

"I guess you need a new theory," Edgar said, enjoying Patrick's look of annoyance.

As they took their seats, Destiny said, "Mr. Crew, I was thinking about the poem that the thief left this time. I think maybe the thief wants to get caught."

"Why do you say that?"

"It's like the poet wants to tell us in the poem that he or she is the thief."

"I agree," the teacher said. "It almost sounds like a confession. Sometimes it's easier to write down things that you can't say out loud. How many of you agree?"

Many hands went up.

Mr. Crew smiled. "A poem is a way to express yourself. Some poetry is called 'confessional poetry' because the poet is really confessing a deep emotion in the poem. You can use poetry to get something off your chest."

Like when a teacher writes a love poem for a custodian, Edgar thought.

"Today we're going to work completely independently," Mr. Crew continued. "What I want you to do first is spend a little time reading some poems by other poets,..." he pointed to his bookshelves filled with poetry books in the back of the room, "and see if you can find any poems that seem to express some kind of deep emotion or say something that the poet may have had a hard time saying out loud. Then I want you to experiment. Write something of your own. And here's what's different: You don't have to turn this one in. You may share it if you want, but you don't have to."

"Can it be deep and funny at the same time?" Taz asked.

"There's always a place for humor."

"If we don't have to turn it in, we could just sit here all period and scribble," Sammy said with a grin.

Mr. Crew shrugged. "I'll take that risk. I want you to experience the idea that poetry can be helpful to you, a way to express yourself even if nobody reads it but you. Go back and pick out a book to give you some inspiration."

The students picked out books and brought them back

to their desks and began reading quietly. Edgar looked around the room. He was dying to know what was on each person's mind.

The room was hushed. The idea of taking time in school to write something that didn't even have to be turned in had a different feel to it. It somehow seemed less like work and more like...real life.

When Edgar was in the middle of his second draft, Taz walked by to sharpen his pencil. He dropped off a note.

> **To Edgar And Destiny:**
>
> **Thanks for the poem**
> **That you slipped**
> **through the slot**
> **I liked the spit and**
> **slobber**
> **I'm glad you didn't**
> **send snot!**
> **P.S. I recognized your**
> **handwriting.**

Edgar grinned. He was just about to pass the note to Destiny when she passed a note to him.

> At recess will you meet with me?
> Underneath the willow tree?

Two notes in one period. And a meeting with Destiny! He couldn't wait.

CHAPTER TWENTY

The closer Edgar got to the willow tree, the more nervous he felt. Could he really tell Destiny his theory about Ms. Herschel being a coffee hog? Would she think it was stupid?

Destiny smiled up at him when he arrived. She was sitting on her coat. "The grass is still damp."

"That's okay," Edgar said, sitting down. Investigators didn't worry about such things.

Taz ran over. "Are you guys talking about the crimes? Can I be in?"

"Okay with me," Edgar said, and Destiny agreed.

"Who do you think is the prime suspect?" Taz asked, crouching down.

Not quite ready to reveal his idea, Edgar suggested making a list of all possible suspects.

"Should we start with just the people in our class first?" Destiny asked.

"Okay," Edgar said, pulling out his notebook. "We need to look at all the walkers. Nobody who rides the bus could do it because the crimes have all happened before the bus arrives." Edgar thumbed back to an earlier page and read the names of the walkers. "We can cross out you guys, so that leaves Kip, Patrick, Maia, and Gabriela as the top four suspects from our class."

"Maia loves poetry almost as much as I do," Destiny said. "But why would she steal her own fish? What about Kip?"

"Kip is fast," Taz said. "He loves candy, so maybe he is selling the stuff he steals so he can buy candy."

"I have been keeping an eye on him," Edgar admitted, and he told them his idea about the skateboard.

"What about Gabriela?" Destiny said. "She collects things, like those wooden animals. Maybe she is stealing to start new collections. The crimes started happening right after she came here!"

"That's true," Taz said. "Very fishy! Ha ha. But her English isn't very good yet. Could she have written those poems? What about Patrick! Maybe he's plotting the whole thing just so he can look good solving it!"

"Interesting," Edgar said.

"I have an idea!" Destiny exclaimed. "Let's put on a play for everybody in our class about a robbery and watch the audience. If the guilty person is in our class, he or she will probably look very nervous."

"Eyeballs never lie," Edgar said.

"Yeah, but wait a minute. I don't see how it can be one of us. We don't have a key to Ms. Herschel's room," Taz said. "Last time something was stolen, the door was locked."

Edgar nodded. "Good point."

"It has to be somebody with keys!" Destiny said.

Edgar took a breath. "I think it's time to tell you another possible theory I've been working on."

They leaned closer.

"Who has all the keys and could easily use the school computers because he arrives here first? Mr. Browning! He is tall. He could mop away his own footprints and fingerprints! And he loves poetry! And coffee!"

"What does coffee have to do with it?" Taz asked.

Edgar told them about the coffee revenge theory. Even though it wasn't relevant to the crimes, he couldn't help adding the part about Ms. Barrett writing Mr. Browning a love poem.

"Ms. Barrett is in love with Mr. Browning?" Destiny gasped. "I hope he's not a criminal."

"I think we should keep our eyes on him," Edgar said. "Maybe we should search that closet where he keeps his supplies."

"Uh-oh!" Taz said. "Patrick is spying on us."

Edgar and Destiny looked. Patrick was standing on the blacktop, staring at them with a pair of binoculars.

"Don't let him find out who our new suspect is," Edgar said. "He'll steal our information and beat us to him."

"I have an idea." Taz whispered a plan.

They listened. Then, Destiny pulled out a piece of paper and wrote:

> Edgar,
>   We found chocolate smudges on the doorknob of Ms. Herschel's classroom. We inspected these and found them to be fingerprints. We believe the fingerprints

belong to Kip, who is now our main suspect. We also found tracks on the floor. We think he rolled in on his skateboard so that he wouldn't leave shoe prints! Let's focus on Kip!—Destiny and Taz

She slipped the note to Edgar just as the bell rang announcing the end of recess.

As they walked in, Edgar made sure to pass in front of Patrick and "accidentally" let the note slip to the ground.

Patrick saw it and snatched it up. After he read it, he stuffed it in his notebook, and then he went running after Kip.

The three new friends gave each other the thumbs up and rushed into the building, whispering the details of the next thrilling phase of their plan.

CHAPTER TWENTY-ONE

"Patrick! What are you doing?" Mr. Crew stopped the lesson.

Patrick was on the floor, pulling a pencil out of the spiral binding of Kip's notebook, which was under Kip's desk.

"I was just...borrowing a pencil," Patrick said.

"I see a pencil on your desk, Patrick," Mr. Crew said.

Patrick wanted Kip's pencil for fingerprints, Edgar guessed. Their plan was working!

Four times, Kip had to turn around and tell Patrick to stop peering over his shoulder. Finally, Mr. Crew dismissed everyone for the last class, which on Fridays was music. Kip was out the door, followed closely by his new shadow.

"Leave me alone, Patrick!" Kip yelled.

Destiny, Taz, and Edgar walked separately, so that they wouldn't call attention to themselves.

As soon as they arrived in the music room, the team went to work.

First, Taz asked if he could use the bathroom quickly before class. Ms. Schubert said yes, and he hurried out.

Then, while Destiny asked the teacher a question, Edgar "accidentally" knocked her coffee cup off her desk. Black coffee spilled all over the floor.

"Sorry!" Edgar said and offered to get some paper towels from the bathroom.

After he left, Destiny carried out part three of the plan. "Ms. Schubert, Edgar might not bring enough towels. Maybe I should get Mr. Browning and ask him to bring his mop."

"Good idea," Ms. Schubert said.

Destiny hurried out the door. At the end of the hallway, Edgar was waiting.

"Where's Taz?"

"I don't know. He was supposed to meet us here."

"Let's go. We don't have much time."

They hurried down the hallway to the closet marked "Custodial Supplies." Edgar opened the door. At the sound of footsteps coming down the hall, Destiny pulled him into the closet with her and shut the door.

Not again! Edgar thought.

"Maybe there's a light switch on the wall by the door," Destiny whispered.

Edgar reached out.

"Ouch!" she exclaimed.

"What was that?"

"My nose!"

"Sorry!" Edgar found a switch and turned it on.

The closet was large, filled on all sides with shelves of cleaning supplies.

"It smells clean!" Destiny said. "Like my Aunt Mildred's apartment."

"Look!" Edgar pointed out a shelf of poetry books.

"*That's* interesting!" Destiny said.

"Do you see Slurpy? Or Ms. Herschel's iris? Or her fan?"

Destiny looked on the high shelves. Edgar got down on his knees and checked the low shelves. Underneath the bottom shelf on the right he saw something white. He pulled it out. A card.

From: Liz Barrett
To: Rob Browning

"It's the card!" Edgar whispered.

"What card?" Destiny asked.

"Ms. Barrett wrote Mr. Browning a poem and slipped it under the door. The door must have pushed it under the shelf. He never saw it." Edgar turned it over. "What should we do with it?"

"If Mr. Browning is a thief, then Ms. Barrett is better off without him," Destiny reasoned. "But if he isn't the thief and if he's in love with Ms. Barrett, wouldn't he want to know that she loves him, too?"

Edgar put the card, facing out, on the shelf with all the poetry books.

They both heard footsteps coming down the hall.

"What if it's Mr. Browning?" Destiny whispered, eyes widening.

"If he knows we're on to him, he might try to get rid of us!" Edgar whispered back.

"Shh! I think I hear his broom!"

The door flung open and Taz laughed. "Gotcha!"

Edgar pulled him inside. "Where were you?"

"I was doing my job, finding the whereabouts of Mr.

Browning. He is in the kindergarten hallway, sweeping. What did you find?" Taz looked around.

"Poetry books. And a love poem from Ms. Barrett. No stolen merchandise."

Destiny grabbed some paper towels. "Come on, let's go before we get caught."

Taz went into the music room first, followed by Edgar with the paper towels. Destiny went to the kindergarten hallway and asked Mr. Browning to bring his mop.

By the time they returned, the class was singing their warm-up scales, "*Moo, moo, moo, moo, moo, moo, moo, moo, moo.*"

"Were you investigating?" Patrick whispered.

Edgar pretended his ears were full of wax and sang, "*Moo, moo, moo, moo, moo, moo, moo, moo, moo.*"

"I know who your prime suspect is," Patrick whispered. "I'm going to run a fingerprint test on the thief's message tonight. I'll bet on Monday, I come in with the proof."

"*Moo, moo, moo, moo, moo,*" Edgar sang.

On the bus, Edgar finally found a moment to write in his notebook.

> We didn't find any of the stolen objects, but I'll never forget this afternoon. The whispering! The sneaking! The hiding in dark closets! The footsteps! The opening of the door! The paper towels!
> THIS IS THE LIFE!!!!!!!!!!!!!!!!!!!!!!!!!!

CHAPTER TWENTY-TWO

That night, just as Edgar's family was sitting down to their Friday night dinner, the phone rang.

"It's probably Stephen calling for me," Henri said and hopped up from the table.

"No calls during dinner," his dad said.

"I'll just tell him I'll call back." Henri walked in a moment later with a puzzled look on his face, holding the phone. "It's for you," he said, handing it over to Edgar. Then he turned to his parents. "Since when does *he* get calls?"

"Hello?" Edgar answered.

Destiny said hi.

"Oh! Hi, Destiny."

Tubby and Twig looked at each other.

"Do you want to ride over to the school tomorrow and see if anybody suspicious is hanging around?" Destiny asked.

"Sure. Great idea."

"I'll call Taz and see if he wants to come, too."

"Okay. What time should we meet?"

"How about ten?"

"Okay. See you tomorrow."

"Bye."

Edgar turned off the phone and looked up. "What? Can't a guy have a friend or two?"

On Saturday, Edgar woke up early and watched the clock anxiously. He couldn't wait until ten.

Finally, he hopped on his bike and rode over to the school. Nobody was there, so he kept circling around and around the parking lot. On his thirty-seventh loop, Destiny arrived, out of breath.

"Taz can't come," she called out. "His mom told my mom that they have to take Bandit to the vet today."

Edgar pulled up to where she had stopped.

She squinted, shielding her eyes from the sun. "My mom said they're putting Bandit down."

"What do you mean down?"

"They give him a medicine that makes him fall asleep, only he never wakes up."

"He dies?"

She nodded.

Edgar looked down at the gravel that had collected at the bottom of the curb.

"We should do something," Destiny said.

Edgar nodded, but he wasn't sure what was appropriate.

"We could bring flowers," she said. "Or cookies. Or maybe we should make a card."

A thought occurred to Edgar. "People write poems on gravestones," he said. "What about that? I have the perfect rock. Very smooth."

Destiny smiled.

They rode to Edgar's house, and he found the large flat rock from last year's science fair project. They wanted to carve their poem into it, but neither of them knew how to do that. Twig let them borrow her collection of permanent markers, and they discovered that they wrote beautifully on rock.

After they finished, they rode over to Taz's house. The driveway was empty. They parked their bikes and walked up to the front steps.

Edgar put the rock on the first step. Destiny picked some dandelions, wove them into a little wreath, and laid that next to it.

> Bandit
> Brave and funny
> Ready to run and play
> Inspiring everyone to smile more.
> True friend.

On Sunday at breakfast, Edgar's parents reminded him that the Cabaret was in exactly one week. He asked if he could read a poem and invite two friends. "You'll like them."

"Terrific idea," his parents agreed.

"A poem?" Henri said. "Since when did you start writing poems?"

"There's a lot you don't know about me," Edgar said.

"There's a lot you don't know about me, either," Henri said.

It was true, Edgar realized, and interesting. Henri had

sounded a little jealous, and to think that Henri might be jealous of him was a concept that Edgar had never considered until now.

Henri looked at me with something new in his eyeballs: respect. I think he is seeing that I'm not just a little kid anymore. Just wait until I solve the crime!

CHAPTER TWENTY-THREE

The morning sun danced through Edgar's window and nudged him awake. He hopped out of bed and threw open his window. Hello, Monday! Hello, Blue Sky! Please don't let Patrick solve the crime, Edgar thought. Just give me one more day.

Destiny and Taz were both waiting by the flagpole when Edgar's bus pulled in. They were waiting for *him*! He was so happy he felt like singing, and then he remembered Bandit. What would it be like to come to school after your dog died? Maybe school would be a good thing. Maybe it would keep Taz from being too sad.

Taz smiled when Edgar got off the bus, and right away Edgar knew that the rock had helped.

"Taz wants us to be his alibi," Destiny said to Edgar.

Taz nodded. "If the thief strikes again, you can say you were with me."

"Good idea," Edgar said.

As they walked in, Destiny gave him a secret smile.

Edgar was six inches off the floor. He and his two friends—two!—were on their way to class.

They passed by the kindergarten hallway.

"Look!" Destiny stopped.

Mr. Browning and Ms. Barrett were talking in the hallway. She was holding a bouquet of flowers.

"Do you think he gave them to her?" Destiny asked.

Taz put one hand on his heart and sang, "Here comes the bride all dressed in white, here comes the groom with a bucket and a broom."

The grown-ups heard and laughed, and Edgar, Taz, and Destiny raced on.

Kids were already gathered around Ms. Herschel's door, Patrick closest to the doorknob.

"Uh oh," Edgar said. "Did you get the fingerprint test done?"

"Nothing showed up," Patrick said. "Which means the thief must have been wearing gloves. That's why I'm doing the next phase of my plan."

"What's that?" Destiny asked.

"Patrick and his dad set up a trap," Sammy informed them.

"A video surveillance system," Patrick explained. "Ms. Herschel let me and my dad come at 8:00 o'clock. We hid a camera on Ms. Herschel's bookshelf. It's pointing at the door. If anybody came between 8:25 and 8:55 to steal something..."

"Bam!" Sammy said. "They're on camera!"

All the juice seemed to drain out of Edgar's bones. He pictured Mr. Chen in his black suit, setting up the video camera with expert precision.

"Why would a thief come if you're standing by the door?" Taz asked.

Patrick rolled his eyes. "I haven't been standing here. At 8:15, I walked my dad out to the parking lot, and then I went to the media center to wait. Ms. Herschel left for the staff lounge at 8:25 and she hasn't come back yet..."

"Hey, what's going on?" Kip called out from the end of the hallway. He raced toward them.

Patrick's eyebrows went up. "So, you're usually here early, Kip. I wonder why you're late today."

"One of my wheels got loose," he said, holding up his board.

"Oh, I see," Patrick said, but he sounded like he didn't believe him.

Edgar, Destiny, and Taz all exchanged looks. Maybe Kip arrived early, stole something, hid it, and now was pretending that he was just arriving, Edgar thought.

"Ms. Herschel!" Patrick spotted her down the hall. "Open up!"

"I'm coming! I'm coming! Good morning, everybody. We've got double protection today. Patrick set up a camera *and* I locked up." The teacher handed Maia her coffee cup and unlocked her door.

Edgar held his breath. It would be horribly disappointing if, after all this, Patrick solved the crime. Please don't let there be anything missing, Edgar thought.

"The moment of truth has come," Patrick whispered.

Ms. Herschel opened the door, and Patrick rushed inside.

"YES!" he shouted.

To Edgar's dismay, there was a note on the board.

This Is Just to Explain

I have taken
the tea
that was in
the classroom.

Forgive me.
I have
good reasons.

"This is terrible." Ms. Herschel looked at her desk. "Mr. Crew's birthday gift is gone!"

"His birthday gift?" Kip asked.

"His birthday is tomorrow. I bought his favorite tea, which he ran out of on Friday, and had it all wrapped and ready right here."

"I really don't like this thief," Maia said. "That is just not nice to steal somebody else's gift."

Elated, Patrick rushed to his video camera. "The light is still on! It worked! I wish my dad could have stayed!"

"Let's roll it, Patrick," Ms. Herschel said.

Edgar sank into his chair.

Patrick plugged the video camera directly into Ms. Herschel's computer, and she projected the footage onto the screen.

For the first few minutes of the film, the voices of Patrick and his dad could be heard adjusting the set-up. Then they appeared on camera as they walked out the door and closed it behind them. For the next minute, nothing happened. Patrick forwarded the film until Sammy cried, "Stop! I saw something."

The screen went black. Patrick stopped and backed up until he saw movement. He pressed "play."

The video showed the door knob turning and the door opening. An arm reached inside the door and turned off the light switch. The room darkened.

A vague dark shape crossed in front of the camera, and a few seconds later, the shape returned and walked out the door. The door closed. That was it.

Edgar sat up.

"Too dark," Gabriela said.

"That's it?" Maia asked.

Stunned, Patrick turned off the recorder. "Somehow the thief knew to reach in and turn out the lights. He knew that I had set up the camera. But how? I didn't tell anybody." He looked at Kip. "Unless someone came early and spied."

Kip's leg stopped jiggling. "Why are you looking at me?" he asked.

An idea was slowly emerging in Edgar's mind. The thief said, "Forgive me. I have good reasons." What would be a good reason to steal an object and leave a poem in its place? He opened his notebook and wrote down the four items that had been stolen.

Goldfish, iris, fan, tea.

As class began, Edgar let a new theory tumble over

and over in his mind. He scribbled notes, careful not to let Patrick see them.

When math was over and they were dismissed for language arts, Edgar stopped Mr. Browning in the hall for a quick interview.

Taz and Destiny caught up with him after it was over. "What are you thinking?" Destiny asked.

He pulled them aside, made sure Patrick was not listening, and tested his theory out on them.

Their eyes grew wide. "I think you're right!" Taz said.

"But you don't have proof. What are you going to do?" Destiny asked.

"Innocent until proven guilty, dude," Taz reminded him.

Edgar nodded. "I have a plan. But I'll need your help."

"I'm in," Taz said.

"Me too," Destiny added.

CHAPTER TWENTY-FOUR

As Edgar walked into Mr. Crew's room, he was hit with an attack of the sneezes.

"Gesundheit!" Mr. Crew said. "Good morning, everyone! I heard the thief ran off with my birthday gift."

"You heard right," Taz said. "But don't worry. We'll get it back. We're on to the chump."

"All right!" Mr. Crew said. "That sounds encouraging."

Edgar sneezed again. The tissue box was empty, so he asked permission to get a new box from Mr. Crew's closet.

"A new box should be right on the top shelf," Mr. Crew said.

Patrick announced: "I caught the thief's arm on video camera."

"On camera?" Mr. Crew said. "That sounds professional. Did Ms. Herschel set that up?"

"I did!" Patrick said. As he described his surveillance set-up, Edgar got what he needed from the closet and sat down. He smiled at Destiny and Taz. So far everything was going exactly as planned.

After everybody was settled, Mr. Crew began his

lesson. "So far we've talked about the many ways poetry is used. Today, I'd like you to spend some time writing any kind of poem about any kind of topic. Sort of a free-writing day."

"Can we work with partners?" Destiny asked.

Maia threw her a surprised look.

"Sure!" Mr. Crew said.

Edgar raised his hand. "Can we write a play instead of a poem?"

"Absolutely. Plays can be written in poetry form," Mr. Crew said. "The most famous plays—Shakespeare's plays—were all written in verse."

Edgar, Destiny, and Taz exchanged smiles.

"You can work anywhere in the room as long as you're reasonably quiet," Mr. Crew added.

Taz pointed to the back of the room, where Mr. Crew had a beanbag chair, and the trio rushed over. Edgar couldn't help noticing that Maia looked a little disappointed when she saw her former best friend eager to work with them, as if it was okay for Maia to have a new friend, but not Destiny. He smiled.

All period they worked on the script, and they secretly rehearsed the play all during recess.

When they came back in for social studies, they asked Mr. Crew if they could perform it.

"How long is it?" he asked.

"Short and sweet," Taz said. "Actually, short and spicy!"

Mr. Crew laughed. "Go for it. We're all ears."

"That's a metaphor!" Kip called out.

Mr. Crew smiled. "Metaphor spotting! This is great!"

Edgar, Taz, and Destiny took their places.

"Can we have popcorn?" Kip asked.

Mr. Crew laughed. "Popcorn is for movies, Kip. This is live theater! *Shh!*"

As narrator, Destiny was the first to speak. "Presenting 'The Tale of Glurpy' by Edgar Allan, Taz Raskel, and Destiny Perkins."

Edgar added, "All characters are fictional. Any resemblance to any person is coincidental."

Taz stuck his hands out like fins, and Edgar hid behind the door.

NARRATOR (DESTINY):

One dark and dreary morning long ago
A happy goldfish swam inside his home.

GLURPY (TAZ, flapping his hands and using a fishy voice):

How I do love to flap my little fins
For when I race against myself I win!

Taz ran around in a circle, flapping his hands and making fish faces, and then he pretended to win.

NARRATOR:

Next to the fishie lived a crazy dude
Who'd rather read and write than eat his food.
All day he read and wrote poems with such glee.
He wished the world loved poems as much as he.

CRAZY DUDE (EDGAR, rubbing his hands):
I have a plan that is so cleverish
I'm going to sneak into this room and
steal the fish!
In place of Glurpy I will leave a poem
And then I'll take the stolen goldie home.
My students then will find the poem and
read it
and think that poetry is great. Nothing can
beat it!

Edgar tiptoed across the room and taped a note to the board. Then he grabbed Taz by the arm. Taz yelped and flapped his fins.

GLURPY:
Put me back, you crazy dude! Right now!

CRAZY DUDE:
I didn't know that fish could talk back!
Wow!

NARRATOR:
Soon many students read the poem he left.
They loved it. "Poems are worth a little
theft."
From that day on, they read poems old
and new.
The thief was glad. His name
was ... Mr. ...

Destiny paused for effect.
  "Mr. Crew!?" Maia exclaimed.
  "Mr. Crew?" Patrick echoed.

Destiny said her last line. "The thief was glad. His name was Mr. Drew. The end."

"Well. Well. Well." Mr. Crew stood up. "What a fascinating play about a fish named Glurpy and a fascinating 'crazy dude' named Mr. Drew."

The class grew very quiet.

Edgar's heart began to pound. Mr. Crew's eyeballs were looking right at him, and they looked guilty!

"Where did you get your inspiration for this play?" their teacher asked.

Edgar glanced at Destiny and Taz. They both nodded their heads as if to say Go for it. He cleared his throat. "Before I answer that, may I ask you a few questions, Mr. Crew?"

"Go right ahead, Edgar." Mr. Crew sat on the edge of his desk.

Edgar began to pace back and forth at the front of the room. "You don't like coffee, do you, Mr. Crew?"

"No I don't."

Edgar pointed to Mr. Crew's electric teapot. "You make tea right here in your room, don't you?"

"Yes I do."

Patrick interrupted. "I don't see what this has—"

Taz held up his hand. "Let Edgar finish."

"Thank you, Taz," Edgar said. He turned his attention back to Mr. Crew and picked up his teacup. "You made a cup this morning, didn't you?"

"Yes I did."

"At about what time?"

"At about 9:00 o'clock."

Edgar lifted the teabag out of the trash can. "Hmmm. I see it's 'Tennyson Tea.' Isn't that your favorite brand?"

"Yes it is. It's delicious."

"But you ran out of Tennyson Tea last Friday, didn't you, Mr. Crew?"

"Yes I did."

"Did you purchase tea over the weekend?"

"Well...no I didn't."

"I see. Then where did you get this tea?"

Mr. Crew smiled.

"You stole the tea from Ms. Herschel's room, didn't you, Mr. Crew?"

Patrick huffed. "Why would he steal his own gift?"

Edgar ignored him. "You stole the goldfish and the iris and the fan and the tea, didn't you, Mr. Crew?"

A buzz of excitement went through the classroom.

"You're not supposed to make an accusation unless you have proof," Patrick said.

"I know." Edgar smiled. "May I continue?"

Mr. Crew crossed his arms. "Go right ahead."

Edgar nodded. "The first theft occurred on Tuesday, October 2. That's the same day we began our poetry unit. You said, 'how lucky' because you could use the metaphor of the poem left by the thief to teach us about metaphor. Well, you stole the goldfish and left that note for a 'good reason', didn't you, Mr. Crew? It was to get us interested in poetry."

"What a fascinating idea!"

"You love poetry, and you wanted to teach us that every poem is like a little mystery that is waiting to be solved. So you created little mysteries for us to try to get our attention. You snuck into Ms. Herschel's room when she went out for coffee. The third time, Ms. Herschel locked her door, so you asked Mr. Browning to unlock it for you. You told him that you needed to borrow her calculator, didn't you? The fourth time, you saw Patrick and his dad installing the video device, so you waited until they were gone, then you asked Mr. Browning to unlock the door again—so you could return the calculator, you said. And you snuck in, careful not to be filmed. You stole a goldfish, an iris, a fan, and some tea. What do all those things have in common? Well, the goldfish was a gift from Maia to the class, the iris was a gift from you to Ms. Herschel, the fan was a gift from a Spanish student to Ms. Herschel, and the tea was supposed to be a gift to you. They are all gifts. And if you take the first letter of each of those objects you get 'g-i-f-t.'"

Edgar pointed to the message that Mr. Crew had painted on the wall.

A POEM IS A GIFT.

Mr. Crew smiled. "Well. You have quite a theory. But I still don't see the proof."

Edgar walked over to Mr. Crew's closet and opened the door. With a flourish, he removed a sweatshirt that was blocking the front of the middle shelf. One by one Edgar set the stolen objects on Mr. Crew's desk: the silk iris, the lovely black and red fan, and the box of tea.

A pair of black gloves came next. "I believe you wore these gloves to prevent your fingerprints from being left at the scene of the crimes," Edgar said. Then he held out the final evidence: an empty goldfish bowl and a net. "You didn't want to hurt Slurpy, so you transferred the fish to another tank in this bowl. Am I right?"

Edgar's classmates stared at the empty bowl.

Mr. Crew clapped. "Bravo! You have done it! I am the thief!"

The class erupted.

"Where is Slurpy?" Maia asked.

"Safe and sound in Ms. Barrett's tank," Mr. Crew said. "Excellent detective work and a very cool idea to put on the play."

"That was Destiny's idea," Edgar said.

"But Edgar is the one who solved the mystery," Destiny said.

"Well done, Edgar."

Everyone clapped. Edgar looked around. It was as if he were onstage and the spotlight was shining right on him.

CHAPTER TWENTY-FIVE

"Edgar, would you and your fellow actors like to get Slurpy and return everything to Ms. Herschel?" Mr. Crew asked.

Edgar nodded eagerly. He, Taz, and Destiny raced to the kindergarten room. Being the only ones in the hallway made them feel important.

"Well, I guess my fish-sitting days are over," Ms. Barrett said.

She helped the trio put some aquarium water in Mr. Crew's empty fish bowl and then let Edgar scoop Slurpy out of the tank and drop him into the bowl.

"Slurpy and the other fish were very compatible," she said. "Why don't you take along another fish to keep Slurpy company?"

Edgar, Taz, and Destiny thought that was a great idea and chose a gold fish with red-tipped fins named Fred.

When they arrived at Ms. Herschel's room, Ms. Herschel was sitting alone at her desk.

"You solved it!?" she asked when she saw them walk in with the goods.

"It was Mr. Crew!" Edgar said.

She smiled and said, "Great job."

"Hey," Taz said. "Were you and Mr. Crew partners in crime?"

She laughed. "Mr. Crew told me what he was going to do," she admitted. "From what I hear, his little idea worked. He said you all wrote a lot of great poetry in the past two weeks. It also inspired some real forensic studying, especially from Patrick, which was very cool."

Gently they poured the fish into the newly-cleaned tank.

"Welcome home, Slurpy," Destiny said. "And welcome to your new home, Fred."

On their way back to Mr. Crew's classroom, Taz said, "Did you see the look on Patrick's face when Edgar revealed the stuff in the closet?"

"I thought he looked sad," Destiny said.

"Jealous," Taz said.

"Maybe jealous and sad at the same time," Destiny said.

Edgar knew he'd be jealous and sad if Patrick had been the crime solver.

"I realized something sad," Destiny said. "No more thefts."

"You're right," Edgar said. "It's going to feel funny not to have a mystery to solve." But with teachers like Mr. Crew and Ms. Herschel, it was still bound to be a good year, he thought.

The rest of the afternoon passed quickly. After PE, they went back to Ms. Herschel's room for final dismissal.

While everyone was busy getting their backpacks ready for the end of the day, Edgar noticed Patrick walk over to the trash can and drop his crime investigation notebook in with a *clunk*.

The principal's voice came over the intercom, announcing that walkers were dismissed.

As Patrick left the room, Edgar crossed over to the garbage can, quickly pulled out the discarded notebook, and slipped it into his own backpack.

That evening at dinner, Edgar told the entire story about how Mr. Crew planned and carried out his mysterious plot and how he, Edgar, solved it with the help of his friends. Henri didn't interrupt once, his parents were on the edge of their seats, and Rosy was riveted.

"A genius!" his father exclaimed.

His mom planted a red kiss on his cheek. "We're so proud of you!"

Rosy said, "Goo! Goo!"

Even Henri said, "Yeah. Nice job, bro."

Edgar couldn't remember ever being as happy.

After dinner, his dad suggested they leave the dishes for a little while. He strapped Rosy onto his back and they all headed out to the front yard, which was nice and flat, to play croquet. When his mom won and did a cartwheel, they all started doing cartwheels, and Edgar noticed with glee that his cartwheel had improved greatly. Then Edgar taught Rosy how to do a somersault, which made her squeal.

Mr. Timmid came out and laughed and said, "You guys are the craziest bunch I've ever seen."

"Come and join us," Tubby yelled.

Their neighbor hesitated for a moment, and then he crossed the street. There was something so wonderful about seeing Mr. Timmid trying to do a cartwheel that it made Edgar want to laugh and cry at the same time. He looked at his parents' goofy smiles and imagined how much joy they must bring to sick kids every day, and his heart danced with love and pride.

Nothing could spoil Edgar's mood. Even when it was time to go in and do homework, there was a bright side: At least it was Henri's turn to do the dishes.

After Edgar finished his homework he remembered Patrick's notebook in his backpack. He settled into the comfy reading chair in their living room and, while his parents rehearsed the duet that they were going to play for the Cabaret, Edgar opened it up. Page after page of notes about evidence and suspects in Patrick's careful handwriting. Edgar felt a pang of guilt about reading it, but then he reminded himself that Patrick had thrown it away. Edgar kept turning the pages until he saw the poems.

<u>My House</u>
My house sits
with its mouth closed.
You can walk by it
and the flowers in the front say,
"Everything is all right."
But they're lying.
And my house sits
with its mouth closed.

Two Instead of Three
Two instead of three
Doesn't feel right to me
Why can't they stay together?
Is it me?

He read the poems over and over. Could Patrick's parents be getting a divorce? Edgar tried to imagine what it would be like if his dad or his mom left.... It would be terrible. He tried to imagine what the house would feel like, especially if he didn't have a brother or sister. Is that what Patrick was going through right now?

Edgar looked up at his parents. They were both swaying back and forth as they played an old waltz, his mom, strumming on her ukelele, and his dad, pumping his accordion in and out. Rosy, in the Baby Bouncer harness, had fallen fast asleep. When they were done, Twig said, "You didn't play too bad for an old man!" and Tubby punched her in the arm with a smile.

"Hey," Edgar said. "Do you guys know Patrick Chen's parents?"

His mom glanced over her shoulder. "I know his dad from PTA. Why?"

"Are they... do you know if they're together?"

She turned around. "Actually, they separated a month ago."

Edgar was right.

"Does he seem sad about it?" his mom asked.

"I think so," Edgar said.

"Is Patrick a friend?" his dad asked.

"He's in my class," Edgar said.

"Do you want to talk more about it?" his mom asked.

"No. That's okay. I was just wondering."

After assuring him that he could talk to them any-time, his parents resumed practicing and Edgar picked up his notebook.

> Today is the day I finally solved the mystery. I am celebrating. But I am also feeling sorry for Patrick. If every person saw every other person's sadness, then there couldn't ever be such a thing as a complete enemy because how can you totally hate somebody who you feel sorry for?

CHAPTER TWENTY-SIX

The next day, Taz was waiting at the flagpole with his mom and a new puppy! Destiny had already arrived by the time Edgar's bus pulled up. All his classmates on the bus gathered around.

"His name is Boomie," Taz said, scooping him up in his arms so Edgar could see him.

The puppy was a tiny white bundle with a wide-awake face, a wet black nose, and a sloppy pink tongue.

"Say hi to Edgar," Taz said, and he held out one of Boomie's tiny paws.

Edgar shook it and the puppy licked his hand.

"You can come over and play with him anytime," Taz said.

The morning unfolded with the usual mix of deciphering and daydreaming, drudgery and delight. Before Edgar knew it, the bell was ringing for recess, and he was struck with a problem. He wanted to invite Taz and Destiny to meet him at the willow tree, but he didn't know how. Could he just walk up to them and ask, "Do you want to go to the willow tree?" Wouldn't that sound stupid? If they asked why, what would he say?

He carried the problem with him as the class tumbled out to the playground, but then something wonderful happened. The three new friends gravitated toward one another, and they all headed toward the willow tree without needing an invitation or a reason, as naturally as three leaves floating down a lazy stream.

Maia caught up with them, her round face shining. Gabriela was close behind. "I have an idea!" Maia exclaimed. "Since it's Mr. Crew's birthday, maybe we could write him a poem. All together."

Destiny's smile was dazzling.

"Only if it can be funny," Taz said.

Kip popped out from behind the tree. "I heard that. I want in." He held out his bag of gummy worms.

"Don't mind if I do," Edgar said, popping one into his mouth. He glanced back. The playground was a hive of activity—kids playing soccer, shooting hoops, shouting, laughing, chasing—but Patrick was alone, sitting on the bottom of the slide.

"Hey Patrick," he called. "We're planning a birthday present for Mr. Crew. Come on."

Patrick stood for a moment, stunned, then he ran over.

"We're going to write a poem for Mr. Crew," Destiny said.

Patrick's eyeballs, Edgar noticed, brightened considerably.

They sat in a circle under the majestic old tree, Edgar taking the place of honor, with his back against the trunk.

Maia put the pad of paper she brought on her knee. "Where should we start?"

"Let's all brainstorm lots of ideas," Destiny said.

"But first, let's have a moment of silence," Taz said, in perfect imitation of Mr. Crew. "Silence is the water that helps your imagination to grow."

Gabriela giggled.

Edgar closed his eyes and soaked in the silence, feeling each of his classmates doing the same thing. The rise and fall of the shouts on the playground sounded far away. Above him came the gentle tweeting of one bird to another. A light breeze was blowing, tickling the hair on the back of his neck and rustling the leaves of the willow tree. He imagined the breeze entering in with his breath, swirling and floating and zipping around inside him. This is happiness, Edgar thought.

He was the first to begin.

AUTHOR'S NOTE

Dear Reader,
Here are a few more mysteries to solve. Don't peek at the answers.
—Mary Amato

1. Which famous poet and writer is Edgar Allan named after?
2. Mr. Browning, the custodian, and Ms. Barrett, the kindergarten teacher, have famous names. Who were the real Mr. Browning and Ms. Barrett and what were they known for?
3. In chapter eighteen, when Mr. Crew sees the kids waiting outside Ms. Herschel's door, he says "Ah. The huddled masses yearning to breathe free have arrived." What famous poem is he quoting from? Who wrote the poem and where is the poem displayed?
4. Edgar and Destiny write a poem on a stone memorializing Bandit. What is a poem written on a tombstone called?
5. Authors carefully choose details within the story to match or to amplify the themes of the book. What did I choose as the project for Edgar's class to work on in art? Why did I choose this?
6. What is the name of Mr. Crew's favorite tea and why is it significant?

BONUS MYSTERY

Do any of the thief's poems sound familiar to you? The thief "stole" the beginnings of four famous poems by four famous American poets and wrote parodies of these poems. Find the four poems and the name of each poet. Then write the first initial of each poet's first name (in the order that the poems appear in the book). What do the letters spell?!

ANSWERS TO 1-6:

1. The famous poet Edgar is named after is Edgar Allan Poe.
2. The real Robert Browning and Elizabeth Barrett were famous poets who were madly in love with one another.
3. The poem that Mr. Crew quoted in chapter eighteen is called "The New Colossus," written by Emma Lazarus. It is engraved inside the pedestal of the Statue of Liberty.
4. A poem written on a tombstone is called an epitaph.
5. The art project was to make masks. This was a good choice for this story because masks hide true identities and are often associated with secrets and mysteries.
6. Mr. Crew's favorite tea is called Tennyson Tea, named after the poet Alfred, Lord Tennyson.

ANSWERS TO THE BONUS MYSTERY

"Thief," the first poem, is based on "Fog" by Carl Sandburg.

"Stopping by This Room on a Rainy Morning," the second poem, is based on "Stopping by Woods on a Snowy Evening" by Robert Frost.

"I'm the Thief! Who are You?," the third poem, is based on "I'm Nobody! Who are You?" by Emily Dickinson.

"This Is Just to Explain," the fourth poem, is based on "This is Just to Say" by William Carlos Williams.

    C for Carl Sandburg, **R** for Robert Frost, **E** for Emily Dickinson, and **W** for William Carlos Williams. C-R-E-W! It spells the last name of the thief, Mr. Crew!

FINAL NOTE

Remember, a poem is a gift. So write a lot of poems and share them with the friends and family in your life.